Total-E-Bo

War
Famine
Death

The Beasor Chronicles
Gypsies
Tramps

Out of Light into Darkness
From Slavery to Freedom
The Vanguard
Two for One
Ninja Cupcakes

Home

NO GOING HOME

T.A. CHASE

No Going Home
ISBN # 978-1-78184-560-8

Interior text design by Claire Siemaszkiewicz
Total-E-Bound Publishing

Published in 2013 by Total-E-Bound Publishing, Think Tank, Ruston Way, Lincoln, LN6 7FL, United Kingdom.

Total-E-Bound Publishing is an imprint of Total-E-Ntwined Limited.

NO GOING HOME

Dedication

Thanks to all of my readers who have come to love Les and Randy. I hope you enjoy it as much this time as you did the first time. Thanks to my editor for making the story better.

Chapter One

"Damn horse," Randy Hersch muttered as he shifted, trying to find a comfortable spot in the seat of his truck. His body ached, he wanted to stop and rest for a while. He'd spent the last two weeks in hospital, and he had a sudden urge to go back to the Rocking H and see his family. He hadn't called to let his sister know he was injured or that he was coming home.

He stopped the truck at the beginning of the driveway and stared at the buildings. The Rocky Mountains proved a beautiful background for the ranch he'd grown up on and had left when he was eighteen. The anger and hate between him and his father had got to the point that he had known one of them would end up killing the other if he had stayed. Randy had left the day after graduation and hardly came back anymore. After getting his leg broken and his body stomped on by an angry bronc, he'd decided it was time for a visit.

It had been a year since he'd last been home. The ranch didn't look like it used to. No longer were the barns painted the dull grey his father seemed to favour. They were the bright blue he'd come to associate with clear Wyoming skies. The windows and doors were trimmed in pristine white. There were three more new buildings on the other side of the main house—he remembered his sister telling him they'd had to build more foaling barns.

It's not home anymore, he thought as he drove up to the main barn, which was filled with organised chaos. His sister Tammy stood in the aisle, directing the ranch hands. He climbed stiffly out of his truck.

"Hey, sis, what's the circus for?" He made his way to her.

Tammy whipped around. Squealing, she raced towards him. He was only able to stop her from launching herself at him at the last moment.

"Wait, girl. Be careful. I'm bruised." He accepted a gentle hug from his favourite sibling.

"Oh, Randy, are you here to recuperate or to stay?" Her gaze traced over his body.

"Staying's never been an option for me, Tammy. You know how Dad feels about me." He shoved his hat back on his head. She wrinkled her nose but kept quiet as he took in the view of spindly-legged foals gambolling beside their mothers.

"What are you doing with the babies?"

Her face lit up. "It's time to pay the rent on those three hundred acres Daddy leased from our neighbour, Les Hardin."

"What does the rent have to do with the foals?" He scratched the velvety nose of one of the mares.

"Les gets his pick of each year's foals. That's what we pay."

"Wait a minute. Who set up that deal? He's robbing you." Randy was furious.

The Rocking H bred and trained some of the country's best cutting horses. Each one of the foals was worth tens of thousands of dollars and it was far more than the property they were leasing was worth.

"Wait, Randy. Don't go off half-cocked. Les and I worked out a deal. Just wait and watch." She pointed to the plume of dust heading towards them. "He's here."

Randy bit his lip and fought back the urge to argue. He wasn't going to treat his sister the way their father treated him. Tammy had taken over running much of the ranch when she'd turned eighteen. He had to trust that she knew what she was doing.

He stood back as a beat-up black truck clattered into the yard. When the tall man wearing a black cowboy hat stepped from the vehicle, Randy clenched his fist and pressed it to his stomach. He'd never felt such a kick of attraction before in his life.

Les Hardin was an inch or two taller than Randy was. His hair was cut short enough to be covered by the cowboy hat. The tanned skin attested to hours in the sun. Les' thin lips pulled up in a smile as Tammy greeted him, but Randy got a look at the man's eyes when he tilted his hat back. Dark brown, and filled with a sorrow so deep Randy was sure he'd drown in it. *Here was a man who has lost everything important to him,* Randy thought.

Randy's dick hardened and he groaned. He didn't want to lust after this man. He didn't want to get involved with anyone near the ranch. Avoiding any possibility of that made his life more peaceful when he did come back. At least, it was one less reason for his father to hassle him.

Those brown eyes turned his way and he realised Tammy was waving for him to come over. Reluctance dogged his steps. Why did he get the feeling this man would change his life?

"Les, this is my older brother Randy," Tammy introduced them.

"Ah, the bronc rider."

Les' voice was a deep honey drawl. Randy's skin tingled where the man's eyes studied the cuts on his face.

"Did you stick?"

Blinking, Randy realised Les was talking to him. "Yeah, made eight. Then the pickup rider screwed up. Dropped my ass right in front of the bitch and she stomped the shit out of me." He held out his hand. "You must be Les Hardin. Heard you bought Old Jake's place."

He fought back the shiver threatening to race down his spine when Les' rough, calloused hand closed around his and shook.

"Yes, I did. It was bigger than I was looking for, but it was available when I needed it."

Something flickered in those sad eyes, but it was gone before he could make it out.

"Good thing we were looking for land to lease." Tammy grabbed Les' arm and dragged him towards the mares and their babies.

Disappointment burned in Randy's stomach. First man in a while he'd been seriously attracted to and it looked like his sister had prior claim. Didn't it figure that some of the best-looking ones weren't gay?

He made his way to where Tammy was gushing over the babies. He stood close enough to listen in on their conversation but not close enough to put a damper on it.

"Tammy, Jackson said to meet him out at the usual place tonight if you're interested." Les' voice was low, as if he didn't want anyone else to hear.

"Oh, he's back from Arizona? How'd the show go down there?"

"We added a few more ribbons to the Black Bart legion. You'll be getting a few calls, I'm sure."

Randy smiled. Black Bart was the Rocking H's top stud. He'd bet half of the year's crop was Bart's offspring.

"Great. I'll get the scoop from Jackson later." She winked at Les and said, "See any you like?"

"They're all beautiful, Tammy, but where's the one you really want to show me?" Les' drawl had become brisk.

Tammy's face dropped. "Sorry. I'll show him to you."

Randy started to step forward. He had vowed to stay out of it, but no one was going to talk to his sister that way.

Les placed a hand on Tammy's arm. "I'm sorry, sweetheart. It's been a hard day and my head's pounding." The man swept off his hat and Randy stifled a gasp.

A streak of white along the right side bisected Les' dark hair. It outlined the slight concave dip in Les' skull, just above his right eye. The man's fingers skated over the scar and the dent, before the cowboy hat went back on.

"Oh, Les, you should have said something. I could have hidden the foal one more day until you felt better."

"It's all right."

"Hide the foal? What the hell are you talking about?" Randy joined them as they made their way to a barn set away from the others. "What's a foal doing in the quarantine barn?"

"Here he is. I hope you're willing to take him. Daddy wants to put him down." Tammy gestured to the closest stall where a large bay mare stood.

"Sally Jane? What's she doing out here?" Randy held out his hand for the old mare to lip softly.

"Here." Les handed him a sugar cube. "I don't usually give them sugar, but I forgot to grab some carrots when I headed over here."

"Thanks." He tried not to think about the tantalising scent coming from the man. Sweat, leather and horse was a cologne he'd always found attractive.

They noticed the little bay colt at the same time. Randy snorted in disgust while Les sighed.

"What's Dad doing waiting to put this one down, Tammy? He isn't worth anything."

The milky white film over the colt's eyes told them he was blind. His front legs were crooked and Randy knew the colt probably would never walk right.

"You were right to hide him. I'll take him."

Randy put a hand out. "Wait. You don't want this one. He's worthless. Blind and crooked legs. You won't be able to use him for anything. It's best just to put him down and pick a different one."

Coldness rushed into Les' eyes and Randy had the oddest feeling he might have lost something he'd never known he needed.

"Can you take Sally Jane as well? This is her last foal. She's too old to have another. I heard Daddy talking about getting rid of her as well."

"Yes, I'll take them both. I didn't bring a trailer, though." There was a roughness in Les' voice. The lines around the man's mouth deepened—pain was etched into his face.

"We'll trailer them over later tonight, after Daddy's gone. Thank you, Les, I knew you'd understand." She threw her arms around the man and hugged him. As she ran out, she shouted back, "Tell Jackson I'll meet him."

Silence reigned after she left. Les didn't seem inclined to talk to him. Randy wasn't sure what he had said to anger the man.

"You won't be able to use him for anything, you know." He had to break the silence.

Les turned to him. Bleakness replaced the cold in his eyes. "Perfect creatures find no worth in imperfect things."

The man tipped his hat to him and walked away. Randy had the feeling Les was talking about more than the colt.

Chapter Two

Later that day, Randy went to the quarantine barn. He knew he'd find Tammy there, loading up Sally Jane and the colt. So far he'd managed to stay out of his father's sight. It didn't really matter—eventually he'd have to face the devil. He'd watched his dad drive away and seen one of the ranch trucks pull up outside the far barn.

Tammy was trying to lead Sally Jane and help the foal at the same time. He eased up beside them and took the colt's halter.

"You load Sally Jane. I'll bring this one."

She nodded and moved away. Randy didn't pick the foal up, all he did was lend support as the little colt made his shaky way after his momma. Randy made sure the colt didn't run into anything and they made it to the trailer without mishap. Tammy was waiting to help load and secure the foal for the trip. When they had finished, she got ready to leave.

He hesitated then asked, "Can I go with you?"

She seemed surprised but nodded. "If you'll drop me off at the old line cabin on the way home."

He climbed in. "Is that where you're meeting Jackson?"

She shot a glance around. "Yes, but don't mention a word of it to Daddy. He doesn't like Jackson."

"What's wrong with him?" He knew his father, and the man's dislike could easily be because Jackson favoured a different brand of whisky.

"He's black."

Randy was surprised. "No shit?"

"Yeah, no shit. Don't you start on me." Her chin tilted at that stubborn angle he knew so well.

"I'm the last to talk about picking who to love, sister dear."

As they drove out to the road she reached over and squeezed his knee. He tried to hide the grimace of pain.

"I'm sorry. I know you wouldn't harass me about Jackson. It's just Daddy's driving me crazy."

"At least he hasn't driven you away yet." Bitterness filled his heart.

"He won't, no matter what. I'll stick through all his bullshit. I'm holding on to this ranch." She looked at him. "You know he's talking about disinheriting you."

"Can't say that'd surprise me." The lengths his father went to in order to hurt him didn't shock him anymore. He wondered if his older brother Rick had suffered the same abuse. Rick had run away from home when Randy was three. Rick had been sixteen, and if their father had treated him the way he treated Randy, he could understand why his brother had chosen to leave.

She pulled the truck into the driveway leading up to Old Jake's place. He was interested to see what Hardin had done with the place. The last time Randy had visited the ranch, it had been run-down, with broken fences and dilapidated barns.

The fences had been fixed and the herd in the fields weren't the mangy critters that Jake had run. There were fifty head of prime cattle.

"What's Hardin running?" He nodded towards the animals.

"He's got Brahma, mixed that he's raising for the rodeo as bucking bulls. He has another thirty head of Black Angus beef and ten head he uses for training the horses. Les' got ten horses." She looked back at the trailer and amended the count. "Twelve horses now. Four are in training as cutters. Five his hands use to ride the fence line and his own personal mount. Then there's these two. Sally Jane will probably be added to the riding herd. Don't have a clue what he'll use the colt for."

She pulled up in front of a huge barn. A fresh coat of paint made the building gleam.

"What kind of horse does Hardin ride?" he asked as they climbed out.

"Look for yourself." She pointed to where a big chestnut brown gelding stood in a paddock next to a smaller barn.

He wandered over to the wooden rail fence and studied the horse. It stood seventeen hands, a lot taller than most of the Quarter horses Randy was used to working with. Long legs spoke of speed, but the gelding's solid body and wide haunches told of power and endurance. It lifted its head to stare at him. There was a great deal of intelligence shining in those brown eyes.

"You're a beauty, that's for sure, boy." He held out a hand.

The gelding reached out an inquisitive nose to lip his hand. He patted it with a gentle touch.

"You always had an eye for horseflesh, Randy. I'll never understand why Daddy doesn't want you helping out."

"It has never been my eye for horses Dad questions. It's my eye for men that angers him," he said.

A deep cough made him turn around. His cheeks grew warm when he saw Les Hardin standing with his sister. The tall, handsome man with café au lait skin who was smiling down at Tammy had to be Jackson. Randy opened his mouth but nothing came out.

Les smiled at him slightly, an understanding gleam in his eyes. "I'm glad you approve of Sam, Mr Hersch. He's my pride and joy."

Grateful that it looked as if Les was going to ignore his comment, he nodded to the gelding. "What breed is he?"

"Hardin Stables Whisky Sam is a pure-bred Hanoverian. It's a warm-blood breed from Germany. They're used primarily in showjumping, combined training and dressage, but I'm sure Sam would be capable of doing anything I asked of him." Les stepped to the fence beside him and stroked the horse's neck.

Randy could see the love the man had for the horse. "Did you own a horse farm where you're originally from?"

Les shot him a glance and nodded. "In the horse country of Virginia, at one time, Hardin Stables was known as the premier breeder of showjumpers." A hint of sadness crept into those expressive eyes.

"Are you going to start breeding again?"

"Not Hanoverians. Those days are over. My partner bought all my stock except for Sam, and I moved out here to try something different."

"Can't get much more different than training cutting horses." He heard his sister laugh. Looking over his shoulder, he saw Jackson bend down and kiss Tammy. Then he noticed Les watching him.

"Is that going to be a problem?" Les' question was direct.

Shaking his head, he said, "Only if he hurts her. Just a little jealous because she's got someone." He clamped his mouth shut. Shit, he never made comments like that, especially around strangers like Les.

"Sometimes it's hard being alone." There was a wealth of understanding in Les' voice.

Impulsively, Randy put his hand on Les' arm. He felt the man tense but he didn't get the feeling Les was going to hit him or pull away. "I wanted to apologise for earlier today. I'm not sure what I said but I know it bothered you. I didn't mean it."

Les looked at him then down at his hand and jerked away from Randy. The man sighed. "It wasn't your fault. In your world, the colt really doesn't have any worth and at one time I was like you." Hardin reached up to trace the dent in his own skull. The gesture seemed more of a habit than one done on purpose. "Things happen to change lives and I've learnt that every creature has purpose, even those who seem least worthy."

"Well, maybe I'm more like my dad than I thought. I jumped to the conclusion that I knew better than you did what you wanted or needed. Forgive me. I should have realised my sister knows what she's doing and can be trusted."

Looking at him, Les nodded. Sally Jane whinnied at that moment and Randy laughed.

"I think we'd better get her out." Randy glanced over at Tammy and Jackson. "If you're willing to let me help you, we can send the love birds away." He tilted his head towards the pair.

Les smiled. "Jackson, I don't need any more help tonight. Mr Hersch has offered to stay and settle the horses with me. Why don't you and Tammy take off?"

"Thanks, boss." Jackson jerked a nod in Randy's direction.

"If Daddy asks—" Tammy started to say.

"He's not likely to even acknowledge my existence, but I don't know where you went."

"Thanks, Randy." Tammy hugged him, before heading off with Jackson.

"Do you and your father really not get along?" Les asked as they went to the trailer.

"Dad would prefer I never come home and I usually honour his wishes." Randy unlatched the gate for the trailer and lowered it.

"Why'd you come home this time?"

Randy handed Les the mare's lead. Taking a hold of the colt's halter, he gave it enough support so it could climb to its feet then helped the foal off the trailer.

"I got hurt pretty bad this last spill. Spent two weeks in the hospital."

Les gave him a once-over. "You're still looking bad, so I'd have hated to see you right after the ride." Les took them to another barn where there were five horses stabled already. "Why didn't Tammy know?"

"I didn't tell her because she would have come to check on me." He led the colt into the stall with Sally Jane.

"Don't you think she might have wanted to be with you?" Les shut the stall door and they stood watching the horses settle in.

"That's the problem. If she came to see me, Dad would want to know where she was going. I'm not putting her in the middle of the problems I have with him. It isn't her fault he's a narrow-minded bastard." He didn't want to talk about his dad. "Can I see the horses you're showing?"

"Come with me. Jackson just brought back the five-year-old colt we've been working from a show in Arizona. He got a third place and came in fourth in a beginner's class." Les led him to a stall four doors down.

"Hey, for a five-year-old that's pretty good."

"We were happy since this was Sue's first show."

Randy laughed. "You wouldn't happen to be a Johnny Cash fan, would you?"

"How'd you guess?" Les pointed to a stocky chestnut colt. "This is Hardin Farms Sue."

Randy got a closer look at the colt. A large scar ran the width of its chest. There was another scar along the colt's neck.

"What happened to him?" He held out his hand for the colt to sniff.

"Here, he's looking for this."

He jumped when Les' arm reached around him to place a chunk of carrot in his hand. He tried to focus on the colt's soft nose and not the warm body pressed against him or the erection rubbing his ass. His own cock filled. He had to fight the urge to push back into Les.

The colt finished the treat and moved closer. Randy cleared his throat, hoping his desire didn't show in his voice. "He's not spoilt, is he?"

Les' soft laugh tickled his ear. The man's chest brushed his back when Les took a breath to answer. "I have a tendency to fall in love easily." A slight hesitation. "With my horses."

"They're easier to love, I think," Randy said softly. "They take us at our actions. Horses don't care what we look like. They don't care who we love."

"As long as we feed them and love them, they'll give us everything they can," Les murmured.

Randy swore Les brushed his lips over his neck before stepping back. Randy wanted to bang his head on the stall door. He needed to get a grip on his hormones—there was no way Les would be interested in him, even if the man were gay. He took a moment to steady himself before he turned around.

Les was watching him with intense interest. Randy wasn't sure what Les was looking for, but he knew he had managed to hide most of the lust the man inspired in him.

"Would you like to see more of the horses?" Les offered.

"No. I better get the truck and trailer home before Dad gets back. Tammy doesn't need him wigging out because the truck is gone."

A look of disappointment crossed Les' face. "I understand. Maybe you'll come for a visit before you go back out on the circuit. Your sister has mentioned you're good at seeing the potential in horses. I'm getting a new one in tomorrow and would like your opinion on him."

Randy wasn't happy about the pleased feeling running through him at the thought that Les might want to see him again. He nodded. "I'd be happy to stop by." He held out his hand for the Les to shake.

It wasn't his imagination that Les held his hand a little longer than necessary.

"I'm looking forward to it."

Randy waved as he headed out of the driveway. Glancing in his rear-view mirror, he couldn't help thinking how lonely Les looked. He would definitely stop by before he went back on the circuit. The fizz of attraction burning in him for Les was the strongest he'd ever felt.

Chapter Three

Disgruntled, Les rode back into the yard. His early morning ride had been filled with thoughts of a certain cowboy. Randy Hersch would never be considered handsome by the standards of the society Les used to be a part of. The man's face was craggy and had seen too many hours in the sun, causing small wrinkles at the corners of his blue eyes. A slight bump in the nose attested to it having been broken at some point.

Randy's body was classic cowboy. Wide, broad shoulders tapered down to a small waist and a tight ass. Les could daydream about that ass...and the man's hands. Calloused and scarred, they told the story of broncs ridden and a life lived.

He wanted to know everything about Randy. What made the man tick? Was the anger between him and his father just because he was gay, or were there other reasons for Randy to abandon a ranch he seemed to love?

So caught up in thoughts of the younger cowboy, Les was startled when Sam stopped and snorted.

Looking up, he almost fell off in surprise when he saw the subject of his thoughts leaning against a dusty red crew cab truck. He couldn't tell if the stiffness in Randy's shoulders was from the injuries he was recovering from or because the man was uncomfortable about being there.

After dismounting slowly, he kept Sam's reins in his hand as he made his way over to Randy. He gasped in dismay when he got closer. Layered over the fading bruises were several fresh ones and Randy's knuckles were scraped and cut.

"I thought I'd stop by on my way out of town. Guess I wore out my welcome sooner than I'd planned." Randy pushed away from the truck, holding his arm close to his ribs.

"What the hell happened?" Les didn't try to stop his hand from reaching out and tracing a livid mark on Randy's face.

Randy closed his eyes and allowed him to touch for a second before he backed off. "Dad and I had a discussion last night. I thought I'd have a little longer at home, but things don't always turn out the way I plan them." Randy turned from him, staring at the cattle in the distance.

"It must have been a hell of a discussion." He tried to be nonchalant about the bruises but he could feel anger building.

"We didn't talk about anything new."

"You hurt your ribs?" He led Sam to the barn where one of his ranch hands was working. Normally he'd take care of unsaddling the horse, but he wanted to get Randy inside and look at his injuries.

"Nothing I haven't done before. I'm okay as long as I don't take a deep breath." Randy quirked a smile his way.

"Hey, Larry, take care of Sam for me." He handed the reins to his ranch hand.

"Sure, boss." Larry gave him a questioning look but didn't say anything else.

"Let's go inside. I haven't had breakfast yet. Why don't you join me? Maybe we could tape those ribs as well." Les wondered if Randy would be open to an offer of a guest room. He didn't want the man travelling by himself while he was injured.

"You don't need to feed me or feel sorry for me." Randy was defensive.

Les understood how being hurt made someone feel vulnerable. "I can't help but feel a little sorry for you. I'm not going to lie about that. I can't imagine having a father who hated me that much." Les moved towards the house.

"Your father accepts you?"

"He did. He was always supportive of my choices and me. He died a year after my accident. At least he was there during the worst part. That's more than I can say for the man I thought loved me."

Randy blinked and Les could tell his statement had caught the man off guard.

"What happened?" Randy's question hung in the air, as if he were unsure he should even ask it. Les didn't mind the questions—he expected them, especially when people saw his scars.

"Sit down. Margie," he called.

Margie was Les' housekeeper and cook. She'd been a part of the Hardin family long before he had been born. She bustled out of the kitchen, bringing two plates filled with food.

"I saw the young man pull up and, since I raised you to have manners, I figured you'd ask him in." She got a good look at Randy's face. "I'll put some bandages and tape in your room, Master Leslie."

He smiled at Randy's raised eyebrows. "Leslie Marshall Hardin the third."

"Quite a mouthful." Sitting at the table, Randy stared at the plate.

"Eat it. Margie'll get mad at me if you don't."

"I wouldn't want to get you in trouble with Margie." Randy dug into the eggs.

"Good. She's a terror when she's not happy." Les was thrilled that Randy had seemed to relax a little.

"So what happened?" Randy nodded towards his scar.

"A riding accident. Sam and I were competing in a Grand Prix down in Florida—a Grand Prix is the top level of competition in showjumping," he explained at Randy's confused look. "Anyway, I had complained about the footing on the landing side of a few jumps. It was too slick, but no one paid any attention to me. Taylor, my partner, rode before me. His horse slipped at one of the fences, as did several other horses. By the time I rode, the ground was torn up and I had decided winning the show wasn't worth risking Sam, so we went out slow and careful."

He stopped for a second, trying to calm his roiling stomach. It'd been six years since the accident but it still bothered him to talk about it.

"You don't have to tell me if you don't want to." Randy's quiet statement broke through the memories.

"My hesitation doesn't have anything to do with you. I find it hard to talk about the accident at times. Sam and I were approaching fence sixteen. It was one where the landing had been tricky all day. After ten horses, the ground was dangerous. We went in with enough speed for Sam to jump the fence safely, but slow enough for me to control our landing—or so I thought."

He stood up and went to the window overlooking Sam's paddock. It soothed him to see the gelding. "We cleared the jump and I thought we were fine. Sam's front right hoof slid. I came off and the last thing I remember was seeing Sam's hoof rocketing towards me and knowing I couldn't move."

Randy's gasp made him cringe.

"Sam caught me right above the temple. The doctors said I would have died if I had taken a direct hit. As it was, I was in a coma for six months. When I came out of it, I had to learn how to walk, talk and do everything again. It's taken me five years to get to the point where I don't need some kind of help, though, when I'm stressed, I tend to have problems with my left side and get headaches, as you've seen."

Randy was silent for a moment, then said, "I guess you're a miracle."

Les smiled. "If I am, it's because of that horse out there. People who saw the accident told me Sam twisted in some way to avoid giving me a direct hit. I thank God every minute I was riding him that day and wearing a helmet."

"Was the horse injured?"

"He wrenched his back and broke his ankle. That's why he's not competing anymore. His body can't take the pounding of the show circuit. So he lives the high life here and he'll stay with me until he dies."

Les turned back to see Randy had finished his breakfast. He saw him wince when he shifted on the chair. Les approached Randy before putting a hand on his shoulder. "Will you let me tape those ribs for you?"

Les felt a jolt of lust race through him at the thought of touching Randy's skin. *Down boy,* he thought. *He's jittery and used to hiding. There's no future in it.*

He led the way to his bedroom in the west wing of the house. He wondered what Randy thought of it as the man followed him into the room. His king-sized bed was made—Margie must have straightened it up when she had brought the bandages. The room was done in greens and tans. One wall held French doors leading out to a patio, where he often sat late at night.

"Take off your shirt. You can sit on the bed or the couch in front of the fireplace." He went to grab the bandages and oil Margie had left.

Turning back, he smiled at the fact that Randy had chosen the couch. It was definitely the safer of the two. His eyes drifted over Randy's chest and Les knew he was drooling. Even the new livid and old faded bruises couldn't hide the chiselled, ripped perfection of Randy's chest and stomach. Tiny, dusky nipples stood out on a lightly furred chest. His gaze followed the line from Randy's belly button to where it disappeared under the waistband of those faded jeans. His cock responded to the bulge under the zipper of those same jeans.

Randy shifted and Les jerked his gaze away. "Sorry," he muttered.

"It's okay." Randy waited until Les met his gaze. "I'm just not used to looking, or having another man look back."

"Really? Isn't it hard to hide that?" He sat down next to Randy on the couch.

Randy shrugged. "It's not hard when the alternative is getting my ass kicked. Either by my father or the cowboys I ride with."

"How do you deal with it?" Les ran his fingers over the black and purple bruise covering the majority of the man's ribs.

"I left home when I was eighteen. I graduated high school and headed out. It had come down to the fact that I wouldn't survive here. Dad would have killed me or I'd have killed him. I don't come home very often, either. This last spill made me want to see Tammy, so I thought I'd try. Should've known better." Randy hissed as Les pressed on his side.

"Right there." Les put the end of the bandage at the top of the bruise. "Hold that end."

Randy put a hand on the bandage and Les leaned closer to wrap the cloth around Randy's chest. He tried not to think about how the man smelt of sweat, leather and earth. His cock stood to attention and he tried to ignore the hard nipple right at the level of his mouth.

Now's not the time for this, he thought. He quickly finished wrapping Randy's ribs. By the time he was done, both of them were flushed and breathing hard. He taped the end. After moving away from Randy, Les tidied up the room. He helped the man put his shirt back on, thinking what a shame it was to cover all that skin up.

He got out a pain pill and poured some water from a pitcher Margie had left on the nightstand. Holding them out, he offered them to Randy.

"What's this?" Randy stared at the pill with suspicious eyes.

"It's a pain reliever. I take them for my headaches. I figured you'd like one so you can breathe easier." And maybe sleep a little, Les thought as he studied the tired lines on the man's face.

"I shouldn't take up any more of your time, Hardin. I better get going before Dad comes hunting me." Randy winced as he stood.

"He'd really come looking for you?"

Randy nodded.

"Why? Is it because you're gay?" He sent a prayer up to thank God again for giving him his own father.

"I never could figure out why he hates me so much. He's been on my case since I was little. He never hit me until after my mom died and then the restraints were gone. I started fighting back. More than one night I spent outside under the stars because I didn't want to sleep in the same house as him."

"Did he ever touch Tammy?" Les moved closer.

"Not that I know of. He cuts her down verbally and stuff like that, but I think hitting a female is a line he won't cross." Randy winced again.

Les knew all the man's muscles had tightened up on him while he was sitting. "My new horse hasn't arrived yet and I'd really like you to check him out for me."

Randy sighed and Les could tell the man was hurting. He handed him the glass and the pill. He headed for the door.

"I have some bills to take care of. Why don't you sit on the patio and soak up some sun? After a little rest, maybe you'll feel better and can head out." He knew once the medicine had kicked in, Randy would be sleeping most of the day. He opened the door before sliding out, and shut it behind him, not allowing Randy any say.

* * * *

An hour later, Les slipped back into his room. Randy wasn't there, but Les wasn't concerned. He went through the French doors and found Randy sprawled in the lounge chair Les often used at night. Smiling, he headed back inside. He turned down the comforter and unmade the bed. Randy wouldn't be able to move if he allowed him to nap in the chair.

Going back outside, he bent down and shook Randy's shoulder. He couldn't help but grin at the sleepy gaze Randy gave him. *What would it be like to wake up to that face every morning?* Shaking his head, he knew he didn't have the right to wonder about that.

"Can you help me get you inside? You'll be stiffer than a board if I leave you out here." He supported Randy as he staggered to his feet.

Randy groaned and clamped an arm to his ribs.

"I know it hurts, baby. I'm sorry your father is a mean S.O.B."

Les lowered Randy to the bed. "Lie back, baby. I'll take your boots off."

Randy eased back and Les quickly pulled the worn boots off. He stared down at the decadent picture the half-naked man lying snuggled into his pillows made. He lifted the jean-clad legs onto the bed. He knew Randy would be more comfortable without those skin-tight Wranglers, but Les wasn't going to test his self-control by taking them off. So he simply unbuttoned them to make him a little more comfortable.

He tucked the top sheet over Randy and brushed a gentle hand over the man's forehead.

"Rest now, baby." He turned to walk out. At the door he turned and looked back.

Blue eyes stared at him. "I like hearing you call me baby," Randy whispered, closing those intense eyes.

Les flushed. He hadn't realised he'd been using that term of endearment. He hoped the drugs would wipe

Randy's memory of that. He walked away, ruthlessly squashing the little voice in his head saying he'd love to be able to call Randy baby all the time.

Chapter Four

Randy woke to the sound of a raised voice. It was one he knew well. Glancing around the room he frowned, trying to figure out where he was. His gaze landed on a framed photograph of Les Hardin and Sam. It had to have been taken at some fancy horse show. Sam wore a ribbon on his bridle and Les was holding a trophy.

Happiness shone brightly in Les' eyes and Randy began to realise just how much the accident had changed the man. There wasn't any joy in Les' eyes anymore, except when he spoke about his horses. Randy felt a pang in his chest.

"Where is he, Hardin? Where's that queer boy of mine?"

He winced at the hatred in his father's voice. He had never understood what about him set his father's teeth on edge. It was more than just being gay that bothered him. Robert Hersch had never liked his youngest son—Randy had known that at a young age. He knew his best was never going to be good enough. He'd lied to himself often, telling his heart that it didn't matter, that he was fine without his father's love. He had his sister and the horses. That was all he needed.

Levering his battered body off the bed, he pulled his shirt on and buttoned his jeans. Randy tried not to think about Les' hands being anywhere near his cock. He couldn't confront his father with a hard-on.

Damn, he couldn't go out there barefoot either, but there was no way he could bend over to put his boots on.

"Damn it, Hardin. Tell me where the fag is. Unless you're hiding him away as your own personal stud." A sly tone came into his father's voice.

Randy saw red. How dare that man bring Les into the middle of their fight? He headed down the hallway, determined to confront his father. He jerked the front door open, but, before he could step out, he was pulled back in and the door was slammed shut. Glaring up at Jackson, he said, "What the hell? I have to go out there and kick my father's ass."

Jackson shook his head. "No. You're going to stay inside and let Les handle it."

"He shouldn't have to. This is between Dad and me." He tugged on the door handle.

Jackson leaned against the door. "It's Les' fight now because your father brought it here." The man pointed to an open window.

Randy moved over and looked out. His dad and Les were face to face in the driveway. A small surge of pride went through him at the black eye Robert was sporting.

"Looks like you've got a pretty good right hook there." Jackson chuckled.

He didn't answer. He was caught up in the conversation going on outside.

"I suggest you get back in your truck, Mr Hersch, and leave." Les' voice was level. He exhibited a calm Randy had never been able to achieve.

His father looked surprised. "Or what? You'll hit me?" Robert laughed.

"No. I'll have you arrested for trespassing and assault. While you're in jail, I'll have my men drive your cattle off my land."

His father's jaw dropped. "Assault? Who'd I assault?"

"A father should know better than to hit his son." Contempt dripped from Les' words.

"So the little weasel came whining to you, huh? He'd never press charges." The smugness in his father's voice made him want to scream.

"I think he would. You can only beat a dog for so long before he turns on you, Mr Hersch. Remember that."

"You can't break the lease." Hersch was struggling to hold on to his confidence.

"You and your lawyer never read the fine print. I have the right to break the lease at any time if I'm unhappy with the arrangements. As long as I am dealing with your daughter, I'm happy, but dealing with a narrow-minded homophobic bigot is making me rethink the deal." Les turned to head towards the barn.

"You tell him he better be out of town by tonight," Robert Hersch said, glaring at the house as if he knew Randy was watching.

Randy couldn't stop himself from taking a step back from the anger and loathing in his father's eyes.

"I'll do no such thing. Randy is welcome to stay here as long as he wants. I promise you, Hersch, if you bother your son or my foreman again, I'll destroy you." The confidence and certainty in Les' voice and stance made Randy's cock come back to life, but it also brought tears to his eyes.

No one had ever stood up for him. He knew Les didn't do it expecting him to pay him back—Les did it because he had the strength to stand up to Randy's father. Robert Hersch gaped at Les then stalked to his truck. Without another word, his father drove away. Les stared after the vehicle for a moment. Shaking his head, the man moved off towards Sam's paddock.

Randy started to go after him but Jackson stopped him again. "I'm getting tired of you stopping me," Randy growled at the foreman.

Jackson nodded towards Les' back. "Let him be for a little while. He needs time to himself."

"He seemed fine to me."

"For twenty-five years, Les had someone to fight his battles. His father protected and loved him until the man died. When he was eighteen, he met Taylor and he let the bastard do the fighting and talking. Well, a year after his accident, his father was gone and Taylor discarded him like a child getting rid of a broken toy."

Randy thought about how apt an expression that was. "So?"

"For six years, Les fought his own battles. He stood up for himself. He learnt to be strong. He's learnt, but that doesn't mean he likes it. It's hard when there's no one to support you." Jackson squeezed his shoulder and walked away.

Randy wandered into the dining room where the window overlooked Sam's paddock. Les stood with his arms wrapped around the horse's neck and his face buried in its mane. The picture man and horse presented told Randy more than any words. Les felt

Sam was the only creature in the world that wouldn't let him down. Randy felt another pain in his chest.

Slumping in a chair, he dropped his boots. He stared at them as thoughts raced through his mind. What possible reason did Les have for standing up to Randy's father? Why did he start a fight with one of the most prominent men in the county over the man's son? Or maybe there was another reason for Les to tell Robert Hersch off? Randy would love to know why and he couldn't understand why the answer meant so much to him.

* * * *

Les found Randy sitting in the dining room, staring at a pair of boots. It had been twenty minutes since Randy's father had left and he'd managed to compose his nerves enough to come and see if Randy was up. He knelt beside the cowboy, putting a hand on the man's knee.

"Randy?" he asked in a low voice.

Unfocused blue eyes met his gaze and blinked.

"Do you need help getting your boots on, baby?" He clamped his mouth shut. Shit. It was one thing to call him that while he was half asleep. It was another thing entirely to talk sweet to Randy while he was awake.

Another blink and a slight smile. "Yeah. I can't bend over real well at the moment."

Les took Randy's foot and placed it on his thigh. Sliding on a boot, he pulled the pant leg down over it. He did the same with the other then looked up to see Randy staring down at him. Without thought, he rose up on his knees and cupped Randy's face.

Randy tensed, but didn't push him away. Les tried not to listen to a voice saying it wasn't a good idea.

Les leant forwards and gently pressed his lips to those cut lips. Randy didn't join in at first. Les swiped his tongue over the seam of Randy's mouth and a gasp allowed him access to the inside. He made a foray with his tongue into Randy's warmth.

Randy tasted like maple syrup and earth. Les savoured the flavours while their tongues duelled. He grunted when Randy shoved closer to him, obviously wanting more. His male tang caused Les' cock to harden. When his body demanded a harder and deeper kiss, he pulled back. Randy protested and his shocked gaze met his. He could tell by the hesitant movement of Randy's lips that he hadn't been kissed often.

"Why did you stop?" Randy blushed, seeming to realise what he'd asked.

Les chuckled and brushed a finger over Randy's lips. "Your lips aren't up for anything more."

Randy ducked his head. "Why'd you kiss me?"

He lifted that stubborn chin up and whispered another kiss over Randy's lips. "I kissed you because you're the hottest man I've seen in a long time. Also, I wanted to kiss your bruises and make them better."

"You've only kissed my lips." A flirty gleam came then went in those stunning eyes.

"That's true, but I don't think you're up to me kissing any other part of your body." He stood and offered Randy a hand.

Pulling the cowboy off the chair, Les didn't step back. He let Randy's body brush against his own. He cupped the back of Randy's head and placed his other hand on Randy's small waist. He drew Randy close to him, savouring the feeling of the lean, muscled warmth of the male body pressed to him.

Randy didn't seem to know where to put his own hands—he stroked over Les' shoulders, down his back and settled on his ass. Groaning, Les brought his mouth down on Randy again. This time the cowboy opened without Les asking him. Their tongues slid together with a gentle touch. Les didn't demand or get aggressive—he wanted to learn about Randy and didn't want to scare the kid away.

Their hips bumped, rubbing their cocks together. The moan coming from Randy made Les' cock jump. He waited to see what the kid would do. Randy's hands clenched on his ass and pressed their hips closer. The cowboy's erection was thick and those painted-on jeans left nothing to the imagination.

Slowly Les stepped back, putting some distance between them, though he kept his hand on Randy's waist. Randy's eyes were hazy with desire and his lips were swollen from their kisses.

"You're pretty with that just kissed look, but I bet you're gorgeous when you've been fucked." Les' voice was hoarse.

Shock, surprise and embarrassment passed over Randy's face. The man stepped farther away, causing Les' hand to fall from Randy's waist.

"Um," the kid stammered.

Before Randy could say anything else, a cough came from behind them.

"Yes, Margie," Les asked without looking away from Randy.

"Jackson called from the barn. The new horse you bought has arrived." The housekeeper's voice was bland but he detected approval in her tone.

"Thank you. Would you come with me to the barn to check out my newest purchase?" He didn't want to push Randy too hard.

It had been six years since he'd been interested in getting to know another man before he fucked him. He didn't know if it was the obvious innocence of the kid or if it was the fact that Randy was fighting alone against his own set of obstacles. Les knew all about obstacles and having to go it alone. He wanted to give the cowboy someone to lean on if he needed it.

"Sure." Randy walked beside him out of the house.

Chapter Five

"Why did you stick up for me?" Randy followed Les out to the main barn.

Les winked. "Maybe I wanted you to feel grateful so you'd let me kiss you."

Blushing, Randy felt his tongue try to tie but he knew he had to be honest with himself as well as Les. "I've been wanting to taste you since I met you. All you would have had to do was ask."

"Damn, if I'd known that, I would've just thrown him off my property." Chuckling, Les reached out and squeezed his hand.

Randy laughed but persisted, "Why do it, Les? I'm a stranger to you."

Shrugging, Les stopped outside the barn. He turned to look at him. "Your father terrorised you so much, you left the home you love to get away from him. He has no right to do that to anyone. I wanted to let him know you have someone to back you if you need me." Les put his finger on Randy's lips, stopping his protest. "I'm not saying you need me. I just want you to know I'll back you."

Randy sucked the tip of Les' finger into his mouth. The man's brown eyes widened as he stroked the digit with his tongue. He bit it gently, then let it go. "Thank you."

"You're welcome." Les' voice was rough.

He let a little smile play over his mouth. A shrill whinny knifed through the air. He shot a glance at Les and headed into the barn. An angry scream tore through the building. Hooves hitting wood ricocheted in their ears.

"Shut the door," Jackson yelled as a large, grey horse raced towards them.

Les jerked the barn door shut and Randy reached out. He grabbed the lead rope flapping in the air as the stallion ran past him. He planted his feet and threw his weight back.

The grey's head shot around when its headlong flight was arrested. Its wild eyes rolled as it reared and lunged.

He felt his ribs protest the rough treatment.

Jackson and another man headed towards them. The stallion tossed his head and snorted.

Les waved them away. "Let Randy take care of him."

Randy ignored the other men and focused his attention on the horse. He murmured, making sure the horse had to work to hear him. The grey's ears twitched as he tried to keep an eye on the other men while making sure Randy didn't get close to him.

"Oh, you're a beauty. Look at you. Big and tough. We're all scared of you." He held the end of the lead with a tight grip, but he made sure there wasn't any tension on the rope so the stallion didn't feel restrained. When the horse was relatively calm, he said, "Les, where do you want him?"

"Come back towards my voice. I'll guide you to the stall." Les' voice came from behind him.

He stepped deeper into the barn. The grey threw up its head but didn't bolt as there wasn't any pressure. Step by step, Randy moved the stallion down the aisle. It was slow business but soon he heard Les say, "It's to your left."

He turned his head a bit and caught sight of the open door. The process began again until he managed to get the stallion inside. With easy movements, he unhooked the halter and lead rope. He slid out and shut the door.

Leaning against the wall, he clutched his ribs and groaned. He felt Les' hand smooth his shirt over his back.

"Are you okay?" Les' words shook a little.

"My ribs are killing me but, other than that, I'm fine." He stood up with care.

Les glanced at Jackson and the other man. "What happened?"

"The driver said the men who loaded the stud weren't gentle," Jackson explained.

"It took us ten minutes to unload him and he took off just as you got here." The ranch hand rubbed his thigh.

"Did he hit you, Davey?" Les asked.

"Yeah. A glancing blow." Davey smiled ruefully.

"Okay. Have Cookie look at it. If he thinks you need medical attention, have one of the other hands drive you to the doctor's. If not, take it easy for the rest of the day," Les ordered.

"Thanks, boss." Davey limped out of the barn.

"Good job." Jackson nodded at Randy. "I'll finish up the paperwork on the stud. I'm taking Sue out afterwards."

Randy leaned on the stall door as Jackson walked away. He studied the grey. The stallion was a beautiful specimen. His conformation was almost perfect. The horse would win a lot of shows for Les, Randy thought, once it had settled down. The stud moved from one stall wall to the other. Randy snarled as the grey turned and he got a view of the stud's hindquarters.

Spurs and whips had scarred the grey's hide. The stallion would never win any of the halter classes at the shows. He didn't take his eyes off the stud as Les joined him at the door. "Do you save the ones injured by life?"

He felt the man's shoulders move when Les shrugged. "You don't toss something away because it's difficult or scarred. This stud will have his chance. His bloodlines are the best. He's trained as a cutting horse. His last owner abused his generous nature, so the grey has to learn how to trust us."

"That could take some time," he commented.

"There's no timeline for his recovery. We'll take as long as he needs to feel comfortable around us."

Standing close to each other, they watched the stud. Randy wondered if Les was taking the same approach with him. When Jackson returned to take Sue out for a ride, Randy and Les went to help him tack the colt up. Randy ran his fingers over the vicious scar running the width of Sue's chest.

"You never told me what caused this scar," he reminded Les.

The older man smiled at him from where he stood in the tack room doorway. "An auto accident. Old Jake bought him as a three-year-old from your father. On the trip over here, your father ran off the road. He was fine. So it must be true what they say about only the good dying young."

All three men laughed. The colt snorted as if he knew what they were talking about.

"The trailer was mangled, though, and Sue's chest was sliced open. The colt almost died several times before the vet could stabilise him. Old Jake put him in a stall out in the small barn and ignored him. He made sure the colt had food and water but he made no effort to train or socialise him." Les held out a carrot for the colt.

"He was pretty wild when we bought the place. The guys and I had a lot of mending fences and remodelling barns to do so we left the taming of Sue to Les. Within five months, Sue was ready to be started." Jackson unhooked the halter and replaced it with a bridle.

"Started?" Randy wasn't sure what that term meant.

"Broken to saddle. I prefer to start them, not break them. We got him used to a saddle and rider. Then trained him to be a cutting horse. He's still learning but he's come a long way. I think he has a chance at being a champion." Les flushed.

"Not proud of this boy at all, are you," Randy joked. He slung an arm around Les' waist and hugged him.

Jackson was watching the exchange with a smile and Randy wondered what the foreman was thinking.

"You better head out, Jackson, or you'll be late for dinner. You know how cranky Margie gets when someone's late." Les opened the barn door when Jackson was finished saddling the colt.

"I'm not going to have dinner here." Jackson grinned.

"Got a date, huh?" Les winked at the man.

"Tammy and I are going dancing."

Randy saw the glance Jackson sent him. "I know how grumpy my sister gets when people are late, so you'd better hurry up."

When the foreman relaxed, Randy realised how tense Jackson had been. He walked up to the man and held out his hand. "I've got no problem with you as long as you don't hurt Tammy. I can see you make her happy, so it's fine with me."

Jackson shook his hand. Randy and Les watched the foreman ride off, then Randy made his way back to the grey stud's stall.

Chapter Six

"What do you think of him?" Les snuggled up to him and asked.

Randy looked over the horse with a critical eye. Except for the scarring and obvious trust issues, the grey was a perfect picture of what a Quarter horse should look like, with a small compact body, sturdy legs and a deep chest. This horse was bred to work cattle.

"I think if you can gain his trust, you'll have another great horse on your hands. He and Sue would make great foundation sires for Hardin Farms."

"I thought that when I saw him." Les looked at him. "Don't leave, Randy. You're welcome to stay here until you're healed."

Randy's initial instinct was to refuse the offer. He couldn't impose on the man.

"Do you have some place to be?"

"No. I haven't paid any entry fees for any rodeos until next month."

"Then you won't lose any money."

"No, I won't, but are you sure you want to risk my dad's displeasure?"

Les cupped his cheek and kissed him. "Your father doesn't scare me, baby. He has no control over who I allow on my property or in my house."

Randy rubbed his face against Les' palm. "I think I'll stay then. It'll be nice not to move around for a while."

A smile broke across Les' face and this one reached those dark eyes. "Great. You can help me with Folsom here."

"Folsom?"

"He's free of the prison he was in, but he'll bear the scars for the rest of his life." Les nodded towards the grey.

Randy agreed. "Good name for him."

He glanced around, finally taking in the other horses hanging their heads over their stall doors. "Where are Sally Jane and her colt?"

"I moved them to Sam's barn. It's quieter there and the little guy can work on standing and moving without a bunch of other horses around."

"Good idea. Do you really think the colt will amount to anything?" He asked with honest interest.

Les shrugged and moved off. "Maybe. He needs a place he can explore without worrying he'll hurt himself. There's a small paddock attached to the stall he and his mother use. In a few days, I think he'll be confident enough to do a little exploring on his own. His legs might straighten out on his own. We'll have to see."

Les stopped and held out a hand to Randy. When he took it, Les tugged him up beside him. "Come on. I'll show you the rest of the animals. Then Margie will have dinner ready for us."

"Must be nice to have someone cook and clean for you," he teased as they wandered from the barn, holding hands.

One of Les' ranch hands came to ask him a question and Randy tried to free his hand. Les held tight and wouldn't let him go. A glance from those dark eyes and he settled down.

A strange flutter danced in his stomach. He'd never held hands with another man, not in public—or privately, for that matter. Of course, he thought ruefully, he'd never done a lot of things with a man before. Giving an anonymous hand job or getting a blow job from a stranger never endangered his image as a straight cowboy. All those encounters did was endanger his heart. He had become disillusioned by the quick sex with men he knew but couldn't acknowledge on the circuit.

He looked down at their joined hands. His hand was rough with callouses and scars from the rigging he used when he competed. Les' hand wasn't as scarred and his callouses were in different places. Running his thumb over Les' knuckles, he stared at the differences between them, but the same kind of strength lay in their grips.

Randy thought about his decision to recover at Les' ranch. He knew Les was offering him more than a place to heal. On this ranch, he didn't have to hide who he really was. On this ranch, he was being offered a chance to start a relationship. Something he had never had before. Maybe it was time to stop worrying about what his father would think. The man had made it clear he hated his son, so it didn't make a difference. Fate had given him a chance to grow and learn to live an honest life.

"Randy?" Les' quiet voice broke through his thoughts.

Glancing up, he saw the man studying him with a worried expression. He smiled. "Sorry, got thinking about things. Now where's my tour?"

Les didn't say anything, but Randy could see how relieved the man was by his smile.

* * * *

They headed back to the house. Les had his arm around Randy's shoulders and Randy's hand was tucked in Les' back pocket.

"Randy?"

Both stopped and looked to where Randy's sister was standing on the porch with Jackson. Randy stiffened and pulled his hand away. Les sighed. It had been nice to be able to touch another man without worrying about what other people were thinking. He removed his arm from Randy's shoulder and moved so they weren't touching at all.

Randy gave him an odd look, but he wasn't going to try to guess what the man was thinking.

"Jackson, can I talk to you for a moment? I promise not to make you late."

His foreman seemed to understand that Randy and Tammy needed to talk. He followed Les to the truck to give the others privacy.

Randy couldn't believe how alone he felt without Les' arm around him. Shaking his head, he tried to remind his heart he had just met the man. He couldn't fall in love that quick.

"I thought you'd left." Tammy gave him a hard hug. Stepping back, she touched a bruise on his cheek. "What did you and Daddy fight about this time?"

"Nothing new, believe me." Randy caught Les looking at him and smiled.

Tammy grinned at him. "He's hot. If he wasn't gay, I'd have chased after him myself."

He ducked his head and blushed. Laughing at him, she kissed his cheek.

"Go for it, bro. You've never had a boyfriend. Maybe it's time to get serious," she whispered before she left him to join Jackson and Les.

Randy waited for Les to join him before he went inside.

"Sit down and I'll help you with your boots." Les gestured to a chair in the dining room.

He sat down with a sigh. His body complained about the beating it had got and about the rest it wanted. Les smiled up at him with sympathy in his eyes.

"I've been where you're at. We'll put you to bed early tonight."

Randy shifted when his jeans got too tight for his cock. The thought of him in bed with Les sparked lust racing through his body. His cheeks went hot when Les shot a glance at the bulge in his jeans.

"The thought of bed do that to you often, baby?" Les' hoarse voice clued Randy in that the desire wasn't all one-sided.

"Not usually, but an image of you and me in bed does." There wasn't any point in lying.

Les drew a breath. Randy had been so distracted by the bed comment he hadn't realised his boots were off. Not until Les put his hands on his knees and spread them apart. Randy's head dropped back and a moan was wrenched from his lips when Les' hot mouth traced over his jeans. He'd never wanted a man to suck him so bad, but he knew they couldn't. Les rested his cheek against Randy's hard-on and grinned up at him.

Reaching down, he ran his fingers through the man's hair, playing with the white strands. "He's a fool," he said.

A puzzled frown crossed Les' face. "Who is?"

"Taylor. What was he thinking to let you get away?"

Shrugging, Les backed off and stood up, before leaving the room. Randy figured he shouldn't have said that, but he didn't know how not to say what his heart was feeling.

Margie bustled in to set the table. She smiled at him and nodded after Les. "It's good to see Master Leslie smile. I'm glad you decided to stay."

Randy chuckled. "I think it'll be good for me too, ma'am."

"Margie, you're not bothering Randy, are you?" Les came back. The affection Les felt for the woman showed in the gentle hug he gave her.

"Of course not. I was saying how glad I was that he decided to stay." She patted Les' cheek.

"So am I." Les winked at him.

He was relieved to see Les wasn't upset with him. An odd twinge in his chest puzzled him. No one had ever been glad he was around except for his sister.

"Let me get dinner for you, you flirt. When you're finished, rinse the dishes and stick them in the dishwasher." Margie pointed at a chair.

"Yes, ma'am."

As the two men ate dinner, they talked about everyday things. What it was like riding the rodeo circuit and how it was both the same and different from the show circuit. They found they had loneliness in common—both of them had learnt to find comfort in their own company over the years.

* * * *

Les rinsed the dishes as Randy brought them from the dining room. "I'm going to have some coffee and watch the news before I turn in," he informed Randy. "You're welcome to join me."

Randy seemed unsure, so Les decided to give him a way out.

"You've had a rough day. Go on to bed." He dusted a gentle kiss over the man's lips.

Randy smiled shyly at him as he left the room.

"Your room's the first on the left. Do you need any help?" Les called after him.

"No, I'll be okay." Randy's voice drifted back to him.

"Damn," he muttered, then laughed at himself. Pouring a cup of coffee, he smiled. For the first time in a long time, Les was looking forward to sleeping. He had something to dream about now.

He watched the news long enough to catch the weather. Sunny and warm tomorrow. It'd be a great day to court a skittish man.

He wandered down the hall, stopping outside Randy's room when he noticed the door was ajar. He slid into the darkened room and waited for his eyes to adjust. His breath caught in his throat at the sight of all that lean, tanned skin. Randy was sprawled across the bed—naked as the day he was born.

Les knew he shouldn't be staring, but his eyes traced the line of Randy's back and the curve of his ass. Those long legs were muscled and ended in well-formed feet. Randy's shoulders were broad with a long scar along his shoulder blade. The white tape broke up the golden expanse and Les' fingers itched to test the softness of Randy's hair or the smoothness of his skin.

Randy mumbled and moved his head on the pillow. The bruises left by his father and the bronc distorted the strong slashes of Randy's cheekbones. Les shifted as his cock filled.

Shutting the door as he stepped from the room, he shook his head. What was it about this Randy that made him so irresistible?

He went to his room and headed for the closet. Opening the door, he reached up to grab a box off the shelf. He sat on the couch in front of the fireplace and lifted the top off.

Digging through the photos, he found himself sliding into the past. There were pictures of him winning his first horse show. There was the first photo he and Taylor had taken together. Holding it in his hands, Les stared at his ex-lover. Taylor Lourdin was tall, blond and beautiful. His clothes were perfect and there wasn't a flaw visible. He remembered how flattered he had been when Taylor had asked him out—he hadn't been able to believe such a gorgeous man had been interested in him. They had been inseparable from their first date until the day Taylor had broken his heart.

He'd never forget how helpless and hopeless he'd felt lying in the hospital. He'd been unable to walk or feed himself. His speech had been laboured and screwed up. Les had been thrilled to see Taylor for the first time since the accident. He'd known his world was shattered when Taylor had told him he was going to put Sam down because the gelding was worthless. The horse couldn't compete and couldn't be used for stud. Then Taylor had offered to buy Hardin Stables, since Les wouldn't be riding anymore.

As Taylor had walked out of the hospital room, he had broken Les' heart by mentioning he'd moved out of their apartment and in with another man. A man who was whole, and didn't need help eating or talking.

Coming back to the present, Les looked down to see the photo crunched in his hand. A part of Les wanted to throw the pictures out, but his more rational side told him that would be a silly thing to do, because those pictures represented his life. Even with Taylor, there had been good memories.

As he stood to put the box of photos away, he noticed a slight weakness in his left side. An unfortunate side effect of his accident. He'd done more walking than usual today, so his body was tired. He took extra care getting ready for bed. Crawling under the blankets, he buried his face in the pillow Randy had used and breathed deeply. He could smell Randy's scent.

His cock grew hard again. Rolling on to his back, he slid his hand down his chest and fisted his dick. A slow stroke up gathered some of the pearly drops leaking from the slit in the head of his shaft. A fast pump down and his length was slick. Soon he established a rhythm. His hips started moving and he bit his lip to keep from groaning. Planting the heels of his feet on the bed, he fucked his hand. He closed his eyes, imaging a lean, golden back in front of him and his cock thrusting into a tight cowboy ass. His balls drew up and his climax built until it couldn't be held in anymore.

With a low moan, he shot cum over his hand, stomach and chest. Sinking down into the mattress,

Les felt his body relax. He reached for a T-shirt he'd thrown on the floor then cleaned up and curled around the pillow. He hoped his jerking off would ease the tension in his body enough for him to sleep.

As his eyes closed, he remembered the shy kiss Randy had given him. Yes, tomorrow would be a good day.

Chapter Seven

Today was going to be a tough day. Randy knew it when he struggled out of bed and into the shower. Catching a glimpse of his reflection in the mirror, he grimaced at the livid bruises on his face and stomach. The few scars his skin bore hid beneath the black and blue marks.

After his shower, he managed to dress and head out to the kitchen, where Margie was cooking.

"Good morning, Mr Hersch. Are you feeling better?" Margie poured him a cup of coffee.

"It's Randy, ma'am. I'm pretty stiff, but that'll work itself out." He accepted the cup with a smile. "Where's Les this morning?"

Margie's smile was sad as she glanced down the hall towards Les' room. "Sometimes when he doesn't sleep well at night, he'll sleep late in the morning."

"He has trouble sleeping?"

"The doctors say it's leftover fear from the accident. He's afraid that he'll slip back into the coma and not wake up again." She poured another cup and handed it to him. "Why don't you go and see about waking him? I'm sure he'd rather see you than me."

Blushing, Randy made his way to Les' room. He knocked and, when there wasn't an answer, he pushed the door open. He searched through the early morning shadows to discover Les' bed was empty.

Setting the cup down, he wandered over to the French doors. There wasn't a sound coming from the bathroom, so he assumed Les would be out on the patio. The doors were ajar. Pulling them open farther, he walked out onto the river stone patio and smiled.

Les was curled up on the same lounge chair Randy had napped in yesterday. The man looked to be naked under the light blanket that covered him, if the hint of skin from where the blanket barely draped over Les' hip was any hint. Randy stood beside the chair and inspected Les, pressing the palm of his hand against the erection growing in his jeans.

With the white streak through the dark hair and the concave dent in his temple, one would think Les wouldn't be attractive, but each of those oddities enhanced the man's natural beauty. They were testimonies to Les' strength.

Crouching down, he reached out and stroked a finger over Les' cheek. Les mumbled. Randy cupped his face and leant down to brush a kiss over those soft lips. He'd never used this method to wake someone up. He could become addicted to the slow, easy way their lips moved together. Les pulled back and his brown eyes blinked up at Randy.

"Good morning," Randy said with a soft kiss to the cheek.

"Morning." Les' voice was rough, but whether it was from desire or sleep, Randy didn't know.

"Margie sent me with some coffee. Do you want it or would you rather sleep longer? I can find something to do with myself until you're up." He put his hand on Les' thigh, valiantly trying to ignore the bulge in the blanket covering the man's groin.

Sitting up, Les brushed his hand over his hair and smiled at Randy. "Coffee would be great."

Randy rose and retrieved the coffee. After handing it to Les, he stood with his hand on the back of the chair. The patio overlooked Sam's paddock. The gelding was out grazing. The Rockies made a wonderful backdrop.

"I never get tired of the awe I feel each morning when I wake up to a sight like that."

Randy glanced down to see Les gesturing towards the mountains.

"No matter where I go on the circuit, I still believe Wyoming is a perfect slice of heaven on earth." He smiled at Les.

"I can see why you'd think that." Les flung off the blanket and stood up.

Randy ran his eyes over the impressive form Les presented. A small, elaborately carved medal hung from a gold chain to rest in the middle of Les' chest. His abs—an impressive six-pack—made Randy's mouth water. A dark trail of hair led down his stomach to disappear under the waistband of his boxer briefs. Les' thigh muscles were defined from riding all his life. Randy had always avoided checking other men out, but he knew Les wouldn't mind so he eyed the man's package.

The bulge tenting Les' briefs grew while Randy studied him. It was a nice size erection. Randy fought the urge to reach out and touch it.

"Like what you see?" Les moved closer to him.

"Yes, but I'd like it better if it was naked." He didn't step back as Les invaded his space.

"That could be arranged, if you ask nicely." Les cupped the back of his head and tilted it so their lips could meet. His other hand landed on Randy's waist to pull him close.

Randy moaned as their cocks rubbed together. His open mouth granted Les' tongue access to him. Damn, the man could kiss. Taking his time, Les stroked with his tongue and teased with his teeth.

Randy managed to get his arms around Les' waist to reach down and grasp Les' firm ass. He pulled Les tight against him, grinding his aching cock on Les' hard shaft.

Les wouldn't allow him to take control of their kiss but he didn't argue as Randy continued to rub against him. Tilting his head back, he encouraged Les to move from his mouth to the tender spot on his neck. Thrusting against Les' hips, he groaned.

"So eager," Les whispered as he latched on to Randy's skin and sucked.

"Gonna come," Randy stammered as he writhed.

"That's what I want to hear, baby." Les slid his hand between them and palmed Randy's cock.

Randy grunted as Les squeezed and traced the length of Randy's dick with a strong touch. When Les bit his neck again—still fondling him—Randy came unglued. His hips surged in jerks as he shot in his jeans.

"Les," he whimpered as his knees buckled after coming down from his climax.

Les helped him back to the lounge chair where they cuddled under the blanket. Randy was sticky but he didn't care. It was the first time he'd got to snuggle with his lover after coming. His usual encounters were fumbling in alleys or bathrooms, jerking off then rushing to clean up before they got caught.

He ran his hand over Les' hip to caress the man's cock. Les twitched as he outlined the impressive hard-on barely hidden in those black boxer-briefs. He peeked up to find Les staring down at him. Holding that intense, dark chocolate gaze, he slipped his hand under the material to caress him.

Les shuddered as Randy fisted the long, curved shaft. Sliding his thumb over the slit, he collected the pre-cum gathering there and stroked it down Les' cock to ease the friction.

He pulled Les' head down to his for a kiss. "Go ahead. I want to see you come. I want to feel your spunk on my skin."

Les crushed their mouths together and started fucking his hand. Randy tightened his grip and allowed Les to set the rhythm he needed to come. The cock in his hand throbbed and Les lost his smooth tempo to move fast and hard. Pulling his hand off, Randy urged Les to roll over on top of him. He pressed up so Les would have something firmer to hump against. Les stared down at him in fierce concentration. Randy couldn't help but smile as Les' eyes glazed over and the man pinned their groins together with a moan.

Wet heat penetrated Randy's jeans as Les collapsed onto him. His ribs ached but he didn't say a word.

Les rolled off him to cuddle close. "I don't want to hurt your ribs," Les said when he protested.

"I don't mind. I've never spent time with a guy after we came." Randy felt silly admitting that.

Les looked a little surprised. "You haven't? I could tell you hadn't been kissed a lot."

Blushing, he managed to keep eye contact with Les. "I'm not out on the circuit. It's just easier not admitting being gay, so my experiences have been limited to hand jobs and getting sucked off in alleys. I've never been with a guy." Heat washed over him at the thought of Les being his first.

"Oh, baby." Les caressed his bruised cheek. "It's the most wonderful feeling in the world, but we have time before you leave to do everything. I'm old enough to appreciate seducing you."

"You don't mind?" He couldn't help asking.

"That you're not experienced in lovemaking?" Les shook his head. "No. The furtive encounters you've had enforced your embarrassment and guilt over being gay. Our lovemaking will help make you see there's no reason to hide it. It's just as beautiful as any other form of love."

He sighed. A weight lifted off his chest. Les was still more of a stranger than a friend, but for the first time Randy felt like he'd come home. He traced the medal with a finger. It had a horse and a dragon engraved on it.

"What's this?"

"It's a medal representing St George, who is one of the patron saints for equestrians." Les smiled. "It used to be my mother's. It's the only thing of hers I have besides pictures."

"I don't have anything from my mom. There might be stuff at the house, but I never stay long enough to find it." He wondered if Tammy had anything.

A voice called from the other side of Sam's barn and he stiffened. Shifting, he started to stand up. "We should probably get cleaned up."

"Why?" Les pulled him back down.

"What if someone sees us?" He wasn't used to being open about liking guys.

"All my men know I'm gay. You don't have to hide here, Randy. You've got a chance to learn who you really are." Les cuddled him close.

He shut his mouth. Why argue when it was something he secretly wanted? Resting his head on Les' shoulder, he smiled as Les arranged the blanket over them and settled beside him. He closed his eyes, letting sleep and a sense of safety overtake him.

Chapter Eight

It was mid-morning before Les felt the urge to move. He stretched and his arm bumped into the empty space where Randy had been sleeping earlier. Climbing off the chair, he padded to the bathroom. He whistled while he showered. It had been a long time since he'd woken up so relaxed and looking forward to a new day.

Loving Randy would be easy, Les could see that, but what he had to decide was whether it would be a casual relationship. A relationship where they made love and played until it was time for Randy to go back on the circuit. Could Les let him go with a hug and a kiss to thank the cowboy for a great time?

Towelling his body dry, he shook his head. He doubted he'd be able to let Randy go because it was the first time he'd ever wanted a man since Taylor had walked away from him. He just had to figure out how he'd continue to see the kid while he was riding the rodeo.

Checking the clock, he swore. He had one of the stock guys coming to see if two of his bulls were good enough to be sent to the rodeo, and he'd have to hurry to meet him. He pulled on jeans, a T-shirt and his boots. Grabbing his hat, he rushed out of his bedroom.

"Margie, where's Randy?" He moved through the kitchen, kissing his housekeeper on the cheek as he went by.

"He went out to the training barn. I believe he went to check on that new colt you brought in yesterday." She handed him a cup of coffee.

"Thanks. Is Adams here yet?" he asked, heading out of the door.

"No. Jackson said he was running late," she called after him.

Sipping his coffee, he made his way to the training barn.

"Hey, Hardin." Jackson joined him on the path. "You're out of bed late."

He smiled. "Maybe I decided to play lazy boss and let the people who work for me earn their pay."

"I think you had a better reason to stay in bed this morning." Jackson nudged him with his elbow.

His attention caught, Les didn't answer. In the training barn, Randy stood holding Folsom's lead rope. The grey stud shook, its brown eyes rolling wildly. Randy talked with a gentle drawl, soothing the colt. Slowly, he made his way up the rope to lay a soft hand on the grey's nose.

Les shot a glance at Jackson and raised his eyebrows. Not only did the cowboy have a good eye for horseflesh, he seemed to have a magic touch with horses as well. It looked like Les had made a good decision asking Randy to stay.

They waited until Randy had put the colt back in his stall. As soon as Randy slid the door shut, Les moved towards him.

"Morning, baby." He brushed a kiss over Randy's bright smile.

The kid blushed and those brilliant blue eyes shot a quick glance at Jackson. Les knew he'd embarrassed Randy, but a bit of pride shot through him when Randy kissed him back and hugged him.

"You seemed so peaceful when I left this morning, I didn't want to wake you," Randy murmured.

"Thanks, but I almost overslept." Les leaned on Randy, who put his arm around his waist.

"Overslept?"

"Yeah. There's a stock man coming to look over our bulls. If he likes them, we'll be sending them to a few rodeos," Jackson explained.

Les felt Randy tense. He glanced at Jackson. "Come and find me when the guy gets here. I'm taking Randy to see the cattle."

"Sure, Hardin." Jackson nodded.

Les had the feeling Jackson knew why he wanted the foreman to leave them alone. As soon as Jackson had left the barn, Les set down his coffee mug and cupped Randy's face in his hands.

"Baby, I'd never force you out of the closet. If you want to stay in the barns or the house when Adams gets here, you can. It's hard to take that first step when you've been bruised before for it." The kiss he placed on Randy's lips was a promise.

Randy encircled his waist, grasping Les' ass with his strong hands. Randy squeezed and pulled their hips tight. A gasp burst from Les' throat when their cocks rubbed against each other. The friction from his jeans increased the pleasure.

Les bit Randy's bottom lip then soothed the sting with his tongue. His balls started to tighten and he knew he was close to coming in his jeans. There was no way he could meet Adams with sticky jeans.

Pulling back, he kept his hands on Randy's face. "Baby, I'd love to pick up where we left off this morning but I have that meeting."

"I know, Adams. Maybe if I talk to him, he'll look over your stock with an honest eye. I can help you pick out which ones to show him." Randy's eyes were dazed and his voice husky.

"Thank you." Les knew how hard it was for Randy to take that first step. He took Randy's hand and grabbed his coffee. "Let's go check out some bulls."

* * * *

Approaching the outdoor ring where the bucking chutes were, Randy saw a short, bow-legged man stroll over to meet them.

"Damn. Randy Hersch, what the hell are you doing here?" The cowboy offered his hand. His expression didn't change when Randy had to let go of Les' hand to shake.

"Hey, Dusty. I wondered where you'd gone when you retired." Randy couldn't believe his luck. Dusty Spiess had been one of the few friends he'd had on the circuit. Dusty and Randy had spent quite a few nights drinking and playing pool with Burt, Dusty's travelling partner.

Dusty shrugged. "We bummed around for a year or two. Then Burt heard that Mr Hardin here was looking for some cowboys to take care of his bucking stock. Figured it wouldn't hurt to offer our services."

"Les couldn't have gotten better guys. Is Burt here?" Randy smiled as he looked around. It had been rare at a rodeo to see Dusty without Burt, or vice versa.

"Yeah, he's setting up the bucking chutes." Dusty gestured over to the ring.

"With these two to help you, I'm pretty sure you don't need me." Randy turned to Les.

Les studied him and Randy realised that he assumed he was uncomfortable around Dusty. Les' next sentence proved Randy right.

"If you want to go, that's fine, but I was really hoping to get your opinion on the bulls." A hint of disappointment tinged Les' voice.

Dusty stayed silent, though Randy knew the cowboy was watching them. This was the moment where Randy could take a small step out of the prison he'd found himself locked in. Reaching out, he squeezed Les' hand. "I'll be happy to stay."

He could see a smile in Les' eyes and when he turned back to Dusty there was a smile on the cowboy's face. There wasn't any condemnation or disgust, just a look of happiness.

"Hardin, Adams is here," Jackson shouted.

Les caressed his shoulder and said, "Why don't you go help Dusty and Burt get the bulls ready, baby?"

"Sure." He watched Les walk away.

"That man's ass could lead a saint to sin."

Randy's mouth dropped open and he gaped at Dusty like a fish out of water. The bull rider laughed and slapped him on the back.

"I'm glad you had the good taste to see how great a man Hardin is. If Burt and I weren't together, I'd make a play for the man myself." Dusty gestured in the direction Les had taken.

"How long?" Randy found he couldn't finish the question because of his shock.

"How long have I been gay, or how long have Burt and I known about you?" Dusty led the way, shooting the questions over his shoulder.

"Both, I guess." He followed.

"Hey, partner, look at what the cat dragged in. He was holding hands with the boss," Dusty called out to the reed-thin cowboy leaning over the gate on the bucking chute.

Burt Tackett turned and the ruggedly handsome face broke into a big smile. "Randy," the guy yelled as he jumped off and came striding over.

Ignoring Randy's hand, Burt pulled him in close for a quick hug. "I forgot you were from around here." Shooting Dusty a wink, Burt said, "What's this Dusty said about you holding hands with Hardin?"

"Um." Randy had never been speechless in his life, but finding out two of his closest friends were lovers took his ability to form sentences away.

"Randy wants to know how long we've been gay and how long we've known he was gay."

Burt chuckled. "I can't say for Dusty, but I've been gay my whole life. I've known about you pretty much since the moment I met you. That's one of the reasons why we started hanging out with you. You were so ashamed about liking guys we thought we'd help you out."

Dusty leaned on Burt. "I wondered how long it was going to be before you decided that hiding who you were was more painful than just living your life. I knew you were part of our club after a rodeo or two when you seemed overwhelmed and even scared of the women. Then your fright wore off into indifference." The bull rider nodded at Les who was walking towards them with Adams. "If you're going to stay out, he's not a bad one to hang with."

Chapter Nine

"Dusty, Burt and Randy, what a surprise." Casey Adams grinned at them. The man winked at Les. "Collecting busted-up rodeo cowboys?"

Randy moved to stand closer to Les. Silly really, but he couldn't help the surge of unease running through him. Casey always struck Randy as an open-minded kind of guy, but he wasn't secure enough in himself to not worry about how Casey would react to finding out about him.

"It certainly seems that way." Les brushed against Randy's arm with casual indifference.

The little touch made Randy feel better. "The Rocking H butts up against Les' land and, since Dad and I had another disagreement, I figured I'd recover here instead of rejoining the circuit before the doctors wanted me to." He felt he had to give some explanation.

"You're entered in the rodeo at Kaycee a month from now, aren't you?" Casey asked, his eyes studying the bulls Burt and Dusty were running into the chutes.

"Yeah. I got enough points that I can spot the other guys some without falling too far down in the standings." He joined Casey at the fence. Les stood back, allowing him to take the lead.

He felt a swell of confidence and a wave of confusion. Why was it that a virtual stranger was giving him a chance to prove himself when his own father couldn't stand to be around him? He continued to chat with Casey while he mulled the idea over.

"Do you have anyone who can ride these bulls so I can see their action?" Casey asked.

Randy was surprised when Les shrugged and nodded towards Burt and Dusty. "I bought them, but those two run the show."

"Here James comes now. He's still green, but we're teaching him. He should be ready by the time y'all roll into town next month." Burt pointed to a medium-sized teenager jogging up to them.

"Sorry, Burt. Mr Hardin." James tugged at the brim of his hat and smiled.

Randy studied the man. James had a stocky build and large hands. The bull rider's legs weren't too long, so he should be able to get a good seat on a bull. Randy figured James wasn't much older than eighteen. Casey went with Burt, Dusty and James to get the first bull ready. Randy leaned against the wooden fence. A rush of contentment coursed through him as Les moved close enough to him that the man's hand rubbed over his ass. He felt his face flush.

"Have you ever ridden bulls?" Les' question was casual.

"No. Legs are too long for me to get a good enough grip to ride well." Randy shrugged.

Les leaned over and whispered, "I like long legs. You won't have a problem wrapping them around my waist while I fuck you."

Instantly Randy went hard. He reached down and tried to ease his cock into a comfortable position. *Damn, these jeans had fit fine a few minutes ago*. Taking a deep breath didn't work. Les' musky scent filled his nose and all he wanted to do was bury his nose in the crook of Les' neck.

"You're trouble. I knew it the moment I saw you," he muttered to the man.

Les' laughter carried to the bucking chutes. The four men over there turned around and looked at them. Randy felt his shoulders start to hunch. He hated being the centre of attention. He wasn't sure why—it wasn't like they could hear what he and Les had been talking about. Maybe it had to do with the fact that Les had rested his hand on Randy's hip and hugged him tight to his side while he had laughed.

If he was determined to be proud of who he really loved, he couldn't allow this familiar pose to bother him. He relaxed against Les' warm body, ignoring a voice that sounded amazingly like his father. It was trying to tell him his attraction to Les was sick and twisted. He didn't believe that, not deep inside. Not when the weight of the male hand at his waist made him feel safe for the first time in forever.

Casey joined them at the fence. While the man gave him a nod, nothing was said. Randy relaxed further, putting a little more of his weight on Les.

"Nice set of bulls you've got, Hardin," Casey commented.

"I had some good advisors. Dusty and Burt know what they're talking about." Les smiled at Casey.

Les' grip tightened for a second then the older man pulled his hand away. Randy knew Les did it to make him more comfortable around Casey, but he felt bereft without Les' warmth.

"Yep, those cowboys know cattle. I hear you're working on training cutting horses. You've got a pretty knowledgeable source beside you for good horseflesh. I always thought you were wasted riding broncs, Randy."

Randy's confidence soared at Casey's words. He knew he was a good bareback rider, but his heart wasn't tied to the rodeo. On lonely nights out on the circuit, he'd dream of coming home and raising horses on the land his family had owned for generations. He'd always known it was just a dream. Robert Hersch would never allow him to take over any part of the business, even if it meant the man had to leave it to Tammy. He tuned back into the conversation.

"Randy's been nice enough to offer his expertise to help with my training programme. I've got a couple young horses we've just started. Maybe after you see the bulls, we can give you a tour." Les nodded.

Randy couldn't help but smile when he realised that Les had used 'we' instead of 'I'.

"Whenever you're ready, Burt," Les called. He wasn't sure if the happiness bubbling in him was from being able to show off his livestock or if it came from the fact that Randy hadn't pulled away from him when Casey had joined them. Maybe Randy was getting used to his touch.

The first bull, named Buster, jumped from the chute and halfway across the ring. He broke into a right-handed spin. When James' butt slid over to the side, Buster jumped out of the spin and ducked left. James went flying off. All the men cringed when he landed. Dusty distracted the bull enough for the cowboy to scramble over the fence. Casey helped chase Buster into the holding pen.

"I've always thought bull riding was the craziest sport ever." He shook his head as James and Burt pulled the rope on the other bull, Skipper.

"It takes a special person to climb on a thousand pounds of animal. I thought about it for a minute. Until I watched Dusty get stomped by a bull at an event. He was laid up for four months and Burt wasn't worth shit until he got back. I decided whatever money I could make wasn't worth risking my life." Randy cringed, obviously remembering Dusty's wreck.

Les ignored the others in the arena as he reached out to stroke Randy's cheek. "I'm glad. I don't know if I'd be able to see you hurt that bad."

His heart jumped when his cowboy nuzzled the palm of his hand.

"I'll be more careful now," Randy whispered with a shy smile on his face. "I never really had anyone to care if I got hurt or not."

"Not true. Your sister cares," he pointed out.

"That's different. She cares because she's family." A frown graced Randy's smooth forehead. "I guess that's not true either, because my dad sure doesn't care what happens to me."

"The nice thing about being your age is you can choose your own family if the one you were born into sucks." Les leaned in and brushed a kiss over Randy's cheek.

"Hey, boss, we're letting Skipper out," Dusty warned.

They looked towards the chutes. James nodded and Burt pulled the gate. Skipper shot out and immediately went into a right-hand spin.

"He's got some Mexican fighting bull blood." Les nodded towards the animal. "See the way his horns tip down."

James stuck to the black bull for eight seconds. When Casey yelled at him to bail, the kid went to the right.

"Get the hell out of there," Randy yelled as James stopped for a breath.

Skipper took aim at the bull rider. Both Dusty and Burt yelled at the bull, trying to distract him from running the cowboy down. James headed for the edge of the arena where Les and Randy were standing. Les climbed the railings and reached out to take the kid's hand. He managed to jerk him to the top of the fence before Skipper nailed him.

"Thanks, boss." James smiled at Les and Randy as he jumped back into the arena while Skipper was herded back to the holding pens.

Casey came over. "I like these two, Hardin. Can you ship them to Kaycee next month? We'll try them there and see how they act in front of a crowd."

"Sure I can, Adams. Thanks for taking a chance on them." Les shook hands with the rodeo man. "Do you have time to check out the rest of the ranch?"

Casey glanced at his watch. "Sure."

"Boys, can you take care of the bulls? Randy and I'll catch up with you later."

Randy followed Les and Casey to the training barns. Les hoped Randy was impressed by the operation he was running here.

* * * *

Later on, as Randy headed down the hallway from his room to the living room, he found himself smiling. It had been a good day, probably close to the best day of his life.

Les had shown Casey and him around the barns. Randy was impressed by the quality of the barns themselves—Les hadn't scrimped on building them. The exquisite breeding of most of the horseflesh was better than his father's horses. Of course, Les had more money to draw from. It was obvious that Les had an eye for horses and could see below the surface to the heart of each animal.

Dusty and Burt were just hanging their hats up when he walked into the living room.

"Hey." He greeted them with a smile. "You're eating with us?"

"Hardin wanted to talk about the rodeo stock, so he asked us to join you." Dusty winked at him.

He saw the easy way Dusty and Burt moved together. Even when they weren't touching, he could tell they were a couple.

Les came in and gestured to the couches. "Why don't you sit down? What would you like to drink?"

Randy and Dusty asked for beer and Burt for whisky.

Dusty looked at Randy and said, "Go ahead. Ask."

"How did you survive on the circuit? I mean you weren't out, were you?" The question had been nagging at him since he'd seen them earlier.

"You weren't looking for it, but we were out. I wasn't willing to hide," Burt revealed.

"You didn't get your ass kicked." He was surprised.

"Sure we did, once in a while. The thing is, you can't flaunt it, kid. If you do, you won't survive, but as long as you don't rub their noses in it they'll leave you alone." Dusty settled on the couch next to Burt.

Burt put his hand on Dusty's thigh. "I can't promise the cowboys will never get angry or macho towards you, but ride your horses and stay the same as you've always been, a majority of them won't react. You'll lose some friends if you decide to come out." The taller cowboy shrugged. "They aren't much of a friend if they bail when you tell the truth. We can introduce you to a few other couples and that should help you ease into being out on the circuit."

"That is, if you want to stay out." Dusty leant forward and his gaze was serious as he stared at Randy. "Don't think we're pressuring you into going public, Randy. All of us understand how hard it is to break away from the secrets we think we need to keep."

Les brought their drinks over then settled on the arm of the chair Randy was sitting in. Randy noticed Les had a soda.

"You're not drinking?"

"Some of the medicines I'm on pretty much guarantee that I won't be drinking again." Les shrugged.

Nodding, he turned back to his friends. "I have a month to get my head on straight."

The other men burst out laughing and he felt his cheeks heat.

"It'll be the only thing straight on you, baby, I hope." Les stroked a hand over Randy's hair and smiled.

"Master Leslie, dinner's ready," Margie announced.

"Come on, guys." Les stood, offering a hand to Randy.

"Thanks." He let Les help him out of the chair. His bruises were letting him feel them. "I'm not going to be able to move tomorrow."

"Wait until you get to be our age, kid," Dusty joked as the couple followed them into the dining room.

"Especially if you keep riding the rodeo," Burt added.

"I've seen a few rodeos since I came out here and I'm amazed any of you survive to retire." Les sat down at the head of the table and gestured for them to sit.

"I can't remember when I didn't want to be a bull rider." Burt frowned.

"I never wanted to ride broncs." Randy didn't look up from the steak he was cutting.

"What do you want to do?" Les' question was quiet.

"Raise and train horses on the family ranch." He gave a bitter laugh. "Guess I'll be riding the rodeo for a long time."

"You never know what's going to happen," Dusty commented.

"My dad'll have to die before I get to have anything to do with the ranch. He'll be even worse if I come out." Nausea caused his stomach to roll. He could imagine how that confrontation would go.

"Doesn't everyone around here know anyway?" Les handed him another beer.

Shaking his head, Randy took the bottle. "No. I think things would have been worse if everyone knew. Not all of them are narrow-minded bigots, but some are and that can be rough to deal with."

"My dad kicked my ass all over the ranch when I came out to him," Burt confessed.

"Did he get over it?" Randy wanted to hear that there was a chance his dad would accept him eventually.

"Not really. He was always polite to Dusty when we stopped by, but I knew he wasn't comfortable with our relationship." Burt didn't seem too upset about it.

"It didn't bother you that your father didn't accept the man you loved?" Randy asked.

"Sure it bothered me." Burt looked at him. "Randy, I'm older than you and I've learnt that people are going to feel however they want to feel. Nothing I can do would or could change their feelings. I've learnt to accept that. Maybe someday you'll figure it out."

"I think Les and I come from a different side of the story. It was just my mom and I by the time I came out. She accepted me because she loved me and didn't want to lose her only child. The first couple of times Burt came home with me, she was nervous and uncomfortable, but soon she fell in love with him. Now when I call her, she wants to talk to him instead of me," Dusty teased.

"It was just my dad and I. My mom died in childbirth and Dad never got remarried. To be honest, my dad suspected I was gay before I did. He noticed I had a lot of girls who were friends, but I never dated them. Part of it had to be I didn't have time. I was riding forty to fifty hours a week, plus doing horse shows on the weekends. When I was sixteen, he sat me down and talked to me about being gay and what that meant." Les chuckled. "I was horrified."

"Horrified? Why?" Randy shot a glance at Les.

"At first, I thought he was telling me he was gay. No sixteen-year-old wants to hear about his parents' sex life. It could scar them for life. When I realised he was talking about me, I denied it. I didn't want to be different than the other guys who rode with me. Dad told me to think about it."

"What happened when you did?" Burt asked.

"By seventeen, I knew my dad was right and I told him. He gave me a hug and said he'd be there for me no matter what." Les' fingers went to the scar on his skull and traced the white streak lightly. "He never turned away from me. Not even when things got really bad and Taylor walked out on me."

The sad look deep in Les' brown eyes touched Randy and, without thinking, he reached out to take Les' hand in his. A shot of surprise raced through Les' eyes, but the man smiled at him and squeezed his hand.

"What did Adams say about the bulls?" Dusty asked.

Randy sat back and let the conversation turn towards business.

Chapter Ten

Les shut and locked the door after Dusty and Burt had walked out. Leaning against the wood, he sighed. It had been a productive day. He'd got a stock contract for his bulls that made him happy. After all the work Dusty and Burt had put into the bucking stock, it was nice to see their choices validated. He made a mental note to give them bonuses. He knew he wasn't anything other than a bank account at the moment, since he didn't know a lot about cattle or bucking bulls.

A hand slid over his shoulder then Randy's arms wrapped around his waist. His cowboy rested his head between Les' shoulder blades. Les was a little surprised that Randy was reaching out to him. He figured touching wouldn't be something Randy would be used to.

"Are you tired?" Randy's question drifted over his ear as Randy sucked his earlobe in.

"I'm guessing you're not," he managed to say as the blood started rushing from his brain to his groin.

"Oh, I think going to bed is a good idea." Randy pulled Les' shirt up and traced his stomach muscles.

"Bed? Good idea." He rested his head back on Randy's shoulder, giving him access to his neck.

Randy nibbled along his neck and sucked on the sensitive spot right behind his ear. Randy used his rough fingertips to tease and play with his nipples. He slipped his other hand down to where the thin line of hair led under the waistband of his jeans. Les sucked in his stomach to give Randy some room to unbutton and unzip his pants. The pressure on his cock eased a bit but he still felt confined by his underwear.

"Turn around," Randy ordered, taking his warmth from Les' back.

Turning, Les leant back against the door. He saw the gleam of appreciation in his eyes when Randy knelt before him. Air burned in his lungs as he inhaled sharply when Randy rubbed a cheek against his cotton-covered erection. His hand trembled while he ran his fingers through dark curls. Randy reached up and tugged down Les' briefs, taking his pants with them. The fabric went down far enough for his cock to spring free. Randy made a hungry sound.

"I want to taste you." Randy's voice was hoarse.

Les knew he was clean, but he didn't want Randy to trust him on his word alone. "I don't have a condom." His hips jerked when Randy ran a calloused fingertip up the throbbing vein on the underside of his shaft.

"Are you clean?" Blue eyes stared up at him—determination and trust shining in them.

"Sure I am, but you shouldn't believe me without proof." He thought Randy knew better than to accept anything said by a man about to get a blow job.

"If we were anywhere else and you were anyone else, I'd quit now or just give you a hand job." Randy shrugged and glanced down at the floor before meeting his gaze again. "I'm willing to take the chance."

It was an acceptable risk as far as Les was concerned. He traced a gentle finger over a scar on Randy's chin. "I'm game for whatever you're comfortable with, baby."

"Tasting you is what I'm comfortable with right now."

Les rested his shoulders back on the door and kept a hand cradling Randy's head. He wanted a connection to the cowboy besides the man's mouth on his cock. A groan burst from him as Randy licked the drop of pre-cum welling from the slit in his cock's head.

"Oh," he managed to say as Randy sucked him in.

The man might be a virgin in some ways, but he certainly knew how to treat a man's cock. Les fought the urge to thrust. He didn't want to move until Randy had let him know it was okay. The need was building, though—the pull of Randy's mouth was driving him crazy. The flick of a tongue over the sensitive spot right under the crown of his shaft made him bite his lip to keep from crying out. A quick squeeze of the hand fondling his balls. A caress of fingertips teased the smooth skin behind them.

"Randy," he pleaded, staring down at the sight of Randy's mouth stretched around his erection.

The man must have heard the question in Les' voice because he hummed and nodded. Moving slowly at first, Les started thrusting in and out of Randy's mouth. His balls tightened and he could feel the tingling at the base of his spine warning him his climax was close. The gentle scrape of Randy's teeth against his skin pushed him further over the edge. He fucked his cowboy's mouth hard and fast.

"Coming soon," he warned.

Randy shrugged and swallowed him until the flared head of his cock hit the back of his throat.

"Shit," he cried out as his cum burst from him, filling Randy's eager mouth.

Randy didn't stop working him until he was drained dry. Patting the dark curls under his hand was all Les had the energy left to do after his climax. Resting on the door, he smiled down at Randy. Randy finished licking him clean then leaned his cheek on Les' hip. Les ran his thumb over the bruised skin under Randy's left eye.

A soft noise from deeper in the house made Randy sit up and turn white. Les reached down and lifted the man to his feet. After tucking himself back in his clothes, he took Randy's hand and led him down to his bedroom. Opening the door, he gestured for Randy to enter.

"Are you sure? Won't Margie get upset?"

"She's been with me a long time, Randy. She's used to me, but if it makes you uncomfortable you can stay in your own room." Les wouldn't push for anything Randy wasn't willing to give.

Randy looked away from him for a second. His arms ached to pull Randy close and whisper promises he knew he couldn't keep. Randy took a deep breath and squared his shoulders. Turning back to him, Randy nodded.

"I'd rather stay with you." His cheeks were pink, as if he were confessing some embarrassing secret. "I'm a restless sleeper, though. I don't want to keep you up."

Les pushed Randy into his room and shut the door. Wrapping his arms around Randy's trim waist, he pulled him tight to his chest. "Baby, I don't sleep well to begin with. There's nothing you can do that'll bother me."

He pressed a chaste kiss on those full lips that looked like they were going to protest. Stepping back, he smiled. "I think I should return the favour." Les moved his hand between Randy's thighs.

The cowboy laughed. "You're so sexy, I came when you did."

"Thanks." Flustered, he didn't know what to say. It had been a long time since anyone had thought he was sexy. "How about we take a shower then? You don't want to go to bed all sticky."

"A shower sounds great," Randy agreed.

They headed to the bathroom and, while Les stripped, Randy started the shower. Les helped Randy out of his clothes. He knelt on the cold tiles to tug off the socks and tight jeans. Burying his face in the curls surrounding Randy's long, curved cock, he breathed deep. He loved the musky scent of sex and the tangy smell that was pure Randy. He licked at the dried cum on the cowboy's hip. Randy moaned and Les smiled to himself. He figured he'd be doing some sucking of his own before the night was over.

They stepped under the water. His cock grew hard again as he watched Randy stretch and wash. Liquid beads rolled over sculpted muscles and tanned skin—his hungry gaze traced each path. Reaching out, he let his fingers glide over the scars marring Randy's body. There was one on the square chin. Another graced the left pectoral muscle right above the dusky nipple. A third cut a savage mark on the cowboy's hip. The fourth was the worst and the newest. It tore a wicked, jagged track from Randy's thigh to the top of his calf. Les lowered himself to his knees and kissed the wound from top to bottom. Randy fumbled through his wet hair, stroking the white streak.

"What are you doing?" Randy's hoarse whisper was laced with passion.

"I'm kissing it to make it better." He nibbled the inside of Randy's thighs.

"My ma used to do that when I scraped my knee." Randy skimmed fingers over the shell of Les' ear.

"Did it take the pain away?" The head of Randy's shaft bobbing in front of him distracted Les.

"Not really," Randy gasped out while Les licked the water from the underside of his cock.

"Hmm…I'll have to think of something else, then," Les murmured, swiping his tongue over the leaking crown. He teased the slit, trying to capture as much pre-cum as he could.

"A man has to have goals," Randy agreed.

"Reach up and hold on to the showerhead," Les ordered.

Randy did as he was told and the motion stretched him out for Les to feast his eyes on that slender, toned body. He lifted the leg with the scar and placed Randy's foot on the edge of the tub. It spread him out and gave Les better access to Randy's balls, as well as his cock.

"Are you okay?" Les asked. He didn't want to cause his lover any discomfort.

"No," Randy moaned.

"What's wrong?" Les stood and pressed against Randy, making sure to keep his legs from closing.

"I ache, Les." Randy's entire body flushed. It wasn't just from the heat of the water either.

"Where do you ache, baby?" Les knew but he wanted Randy to tell him.

"Don't tease me. You know where it hurts," Randy growled.

"Oh, I'm pretty sure I can guess but, if you want me to do anything about it, you'll have to tell me." He leant forward and sucked in Randy's earlobe without touching any other part of his body.

"Ah. My dick. Touch it," Randy pleaded.

"Good boy," Les praised him. Sliding his hand down over the ridged stomach, he wrapped his hand loosely around Randy's shaft. "How do you like it, baby? Tight and fast or slow and gentle?" he whispered against a chest muscle as he moved his mouth from Randy's ear to his nipple.

Randy made an affirmative noise, but Les didn't know which statement the man was agreeing with. He took a firm grip at the base of Randy's cock and stroked up fast. Randy's hips jerked forward and his head fell back.

"I think you like it fast and tight," Les murmured and proceeded to pump his fist.

Les slid his other hand over Randy's hip to grasp the tight ass he'd been drooling over all day. He let his fingers play along Randy's crease, learning through touch what made the cowboy gasp or moan. Randy's hands dropped from the showerhead to hold on to Les' shoulders. Les rubbed his lips over the wet skin of Randy's neck. Nibbling along the tendons, he made his way to the dusky nipple closest to him.

Groans and the pounding of the water filled the air. It seemed Randy would be a noisy lover, but Les didn't mind. It turned him on to hear how much he was enjoying what they were doing. His own erection bumped against Randy's hip, his moans joining in with the other sounds.

Using his teeth, he tugged on the nipple at the same time that he stroked the shaft in his hand. He gave Randy's opening a tap as well.

"Gonna come, Les," Randy warned, his body straining between all the spots where Les touched him.

"Go ahead," Les encouraged. Pressing the tip of his middle finger into Randy's ass, he bit the hard nub in his mouth and squeezed the cock in his hand.

All the sensations at once pushed the cowboy over the edge. Randy's shout filled the shower. Wet heat spilled over Les' hand as Randy's hips jerked. He wrapped his arm around the lean waist and pulled him close to his own body.

Placing his lips against Randy's forehead, he whispered, "That was so sexy, baby. I love the way you react to me." He rubbed his hands up and down Randy's tanned back, soothing the trembling muscles.

Turning, Randy took his mouth with a slow and easy kiss. "Thank you."

Les shut the water off and helped him out of the shower. Randy stood, quietly letting him dry him off and take care of him before they finished getting ready for bed.

Climbing under the blankets, Les spooned behind Randy. He trailed his hand over the man's chest to rest his palm against Randy's skin, feeling his heartbeat.

He brushed a kiss over the nape of Randy's neck and murmured, "If you wake up in the middle of the night and I'm not here, check out on the patio. Night, baby."

Randy grunted and they drifted off to sleep.

Chapter Eleven

Randy climbed out of bed and stretched. His ribs protested slightly, but other than that little twinge he felt good. It'd been a week since he'd agreed to stay at Les' ranch and had become the man's lover. Heading into the bathroom, he stared at himself in the mirror. The bruises had faded to mere smudges and the frown of pain creasing his forehead had disappeared. Climbing into the shower, he thought about the past week.

He'd never felt so at home in his own skin. There was no need to hide the fact that he was interested in Les. The other men on the ranch accepted their orientation without question. Randy had asked Jackson about that one night and the foreman had explained that Les didn't hire bigoted men. It didn't matter what their preferences were—if they showed any inclination to violence or being close-minded, Les wouldn't take them on.

The knowledge allowed Randy to open up and relax. As his body healed, he'd worked with the horses. He began to realise how much he had given up by running away from his own ranch. He loved teaching a young horse how to do what it was born for. Les had given Folsom to him for training. It was hard to gain the grey stud's trust, but the bond was being built with small steps.

Leaning back to wash the shampoo out of his hair, he planned the day's schedule. He'd find Les and get a morning kiss. His cock filled with anticipation of those hard, thin lips. Taking a bar of soap, he slicked up his hands with suds. He slid one of them down to grip his shaft and the other went farther to play with his balls. He rested his back against the tiles. Stroking, he imagined his hand was Les' tight passage. He pumped and squeezed, picturing the older man stretched out in front of him. Les' brown eyes would be gleaming with passion. That honeyed voice would be crying out his name as he fucked him hard and deep. Randy felt his climax draw his balls up. Calling out Les' name, his cum splashed over his hands and stomach.

He cleaned himself and got out of the shower. Drying off, he inventoried his injuries. There wasn't a hint of pain. He felt a smile twitch his lips. Les had been gentle with him the last week, letting the wounds heal, but tonight was going to be their first time together, Randy decided. They'd done a lot of other things—rubbing, sucking and jerking off, but he was ready for the next step.

Making his way to the kitchen, he found Margie dishing out breakfast. He leant down and gave the housekeeper a kiss while stealing a piece of bacon.

"I'll have your plate ready in a second, Master Randy." She swatted his hand away.

"Now, Margie, what did I tell you about calling me that?" He didn't like her attaching 'Master' to his name.

"I know, but you're important to Master Leslie and I'll treat you with respect." Her tone told him she wasn't going to budge.

"Okay," he sighed. "Can you make Les' favourite dinner tonight?"

A knowing look came into her eyes and he knew he was blushing. "Something special happening?"

"Maybe, and it's not any of your business, you nosey old woman," he teased.

"I'll make sure dinner's perfect. Here's your breakfast. Take Master Leslie's plate with you. He's in his office." She handed him two plates overflowing with food.

"Thanks." He winked at her as he headed down the hallway.

After pushing the door to the office open, he stood watching Les for a moment. *The bills must be driving him crazy,* he thought, seeing Les run his hands through his short, dark hair. When a frown formed between his brows, Randy knew it was time to interrupt the morning accounting.

"Looks like you could use a break," he announced as he made his way to the desk.

Les looked up and smiled. Piling all the papers to one side, the man made room for the plates. Randy set them down then leaned in for his morning kiss. He sighed when their lips met. There was something about Les' lips on his that made him feel more cared for than he'd ever felt before. He nibbled his way along the bottom lip, sucking on it. He slid his tongue in to find the minty taste of Les' toothpaste.

A cough sounded behind him and startled him. Jumping slightly, he fell into Les' lap. Les chuckled and tugged him so he was sitting on the man's legs. His face burned with embarrassment as he turned to see his sister standing in the doorway. She held three sets of silverware and a plate of food for herself.

Winking at him, she came and pulled a chair up to the desk. "Sorry, Randy. I didn't know you were busy."

He didn't know what to say. He'd never been caught making out with a guy. He wanted to scramble off Les and find his own chair, but Les' arms held him tight. Peeking up at the man, he saw understanding gleaming in those brown eyes that stared down at him. Suddenly, he didn't want to move. Wiggling to find a comfortable position on Les' lap caused the man to stiffen and Randy felt a private thrill knowing he was the one making Les hard. When he was finished, he'd found a spot where his ass rested on Les' erection and, whenever he moved, he rubbed against the bulge, drawing low growls from his lover. Tammy watched them with knowing eyes and, for the first time, Randy didn't feel ashamed.

"What are you doing here?" he asked his sister as he pulled his plate to him. After tearing off a piece of bacon, he held it up to Les' mouth.

"I stopped by to see if Jackson wanted to take some horses out for a ride. It's a beautiful day."

Happiness was an emotion he wanted to see more often on his sister's face, he decided.

Les nipped his fingers while taking the bacon. After swallowing, his lover said, "He went into town to place a feed order for me, but he should be back any minute now. I don't know what else he might have planned—I don't see why you shouldn't be able to take off for a while."

"Great." She went on to ask Les about some of the horses.

Randy leant back against Les' chest and fed the man pieces of eggs and bacon while they chatted. A few minutes later, the front door crashed open and they heard boots stomping down the hall. Looking up, they saw Jackson standing in the doorway and the anger on his face made Randy shrink back.

"What happened?" Tammy went over to the foreman and put her hand on his arm.

Randy climbed to his feet and moved out from behind the desk as Les joined them.

"Skinner at the feed store did it again," Jackson growled.

"This is the third time. What excuse did he give you today?" Les' jaw clenched and Randy could see he was getting mad.

"His assistant didn't give him the right information. So I went to the new feed store in Cleary and placed an order there." Jackson shook his head. "They were cheaper and didn't give me the hassle Skinner does."

"Good. I'll go into town and settle our account with the man." Les turned to Randy. "Do you want to ride into town with me?"

Randy wasn't sure about seeing the townspeople. He hadn't talked to any of them since he'd moved onto Les' ranch—he didn't want to hear the rumours that could be flying around about him and Les. His lover wouldn't push him to go and that made up his mind. He had to start facing people if he wanted to stay honest to himself.

"Yeah, I'll go with you." He followed Les out of the room.

"Stop by Sally's if you get a chance. She's been asking me about you," Tammy yelled after them.

"What sort of problems is Skinner causing you?" he asked as they climbed into Les' truck.

"The first time our order came in wrong. The feed wasn't the right stuff for any of the animals. So we had to reorder and we came close to running out of food. The second time the order wasn't even placed. When Jackson and the men went to pick it up, it hadn't come in. Skinner told us he was having trouble with his suppliers so I checked with them. They were shipping everything on time and they hadn't gotten an order from the man for my feed. I don't know what the problem was this time, but there won't be a next time. I'm done dealing with the man." Les gripped the steering wheel with white-knuckled strength.

"I wonder why he'd do that." The Skinner Randy remembered was an old, cantankerous man who complained about everything. That man wouldn't have screwed up orders on purpose because of the pride he had in his store.

"At first, I thought maybe he had a problem with Jackson. So I went in and placed the second order. Then, when it came in wrong, I thought maybe it was homosexuals he hated. Now I have no idea what's stuck up his ass about my ranch and me. It doesn't matter anymore. Jackson found the other feed store. It's not that much farther away, so we'll go there from now on." Les thumped the wheel with his fist.

"I thought maybe it had something to do with me," Randy admitted.

"No, it started long before you got back, baby. So don't blame yourself." Les stroked his hand over Randy's thigh.

Randy nodded. "You weren't in bed when I got up this morning."

"I woke up about four and couldn't go back to sleep. So I went for a ride on Sam and then did some paperwork." Les grimaced.

"Wake me up next time, Les. I don't mind." Placing his hand over the one resting on his thigh, he squeezed.

"You shouldn't miss sleep when the memories get too hard to forget." Les shrugged.

They pulled up outside the feed store. Without thinking about who might be watching, Randy cupped Les' face and turned the man's gaze towards him. He pressed a quick kiss to Les' lips.

"I think it's time we start making new memories to replace the ones keeping you awake at night." He caressed the stubble-roughened skin and smiled.

"I think that's a good idea," Les agreed as they climbed out of the vehicle.

Randy hung back as they walked into the store. He wanted to watch Les in action.

The wizened man at the counter glared up at Les as he approached him. "My assistant gave me the wrong information. Your new order will be here next week."

Les shook his head. "You can cancel that. I want a complete history on my account. My payments have always been on time and I haven't yet gotten a correct order. I'd like to settle my bills with you so you can close my account. I'll be getting my feed from another store."

"Now wait a minute, Hardin. One or two innocent mistakes shouldn't get you upset enough to quit doing business with me." Skinner's face paled.

Les knew the old man realised how much money he'd be losing by Les not ordering from him. "I don't know how innocent they were, Skinner. But three orders and three fuck-ups tell me you don't value my business. I'm going to a store that'll take care of me without screwing me over."

"From what I hear, you don't mind—" The old man never finished his sentence.

Les leaned over and grabbed his collar. Picking the man up, he dragged him over the counter until their faces almost touched. "If you want to keep what few teeth you have in your face, I suggest you never say what you were about to say." He pushed Skinner back and the owner stumbled. "Is that why you've never gotten any of my orders right?"

"No." Peter, Skinner's grandson, came up to the counter. "You bought Old Jake's place out from under Grandpa Samson. He's resented you since you got here. If I thought he had the brains for it, I'd say he's been trying to run you off." Peter glared at his grandfather.

"Thank you, Peter. It's nice to know someone's honest around here." Les held out his hand to the man. "Are you any good with numbers and accounting?"

"Yes, sir. I do the books here at the store." Peter shook Les' hand with a firm grip.

"If you ever decide to dump this job, give me a call. I'm sure we can find some accounting work out at the ranch." Les turned to find Randy standing slightly behind him. "Do you two know each other?"

Randy smiled and Les saw some of the uneasiness Randy had been feeling disappear.

"We went to school together. Good to see you again, Peter." Randy shook Peter's hand.

Les watched the way Peter held onto Randy's hand. Skinner's grandson was checking Randy out. *Interesting,* Les thought.

"I'm glad to see you back, Randy. I asked Tammy when you'd be coming into town. She said you were healing up after getting stomped by a bronc." Peter's cheeks pinked a little.

"Yeah. Les was nice enough to let me stay with him, since Dad kicked me off the ranch again," Randy commented with a rueful grin.

Les trailed a hand over Randy's shoulder, letting Peter know his prior claim to the cowboy. Randy shot him a smouldering wink and Peter nodded.

"Come on, Les. I've got a craving for some of Sally's apple pie." Randy grabbed his hand and started to tug him from the store.

"Peter, that offer's open-ended and you're always welcome to visit whenever you want," Les called to Peter. He glared at Skinner. "I want Peter to do up a final bill for me. I trust him not to fudge the numbers and charge me more than I should be paying." He followed Randy out of the door without waiting to hear what Skinner had to say.

Chapter Twelve

"I thought you were going to punch Skinner," Randy burst out as he walked towards Sally's Diner.

"I've met people like Skinner all over the world. Taylor used to just laugh and walk away." Les shrugged. "Comments like that make me mad and I don't see the point of hiding that fact."

Randy touched Les' arm and squeezed. "I'm not complaining. Skinner has never liked me. I didn't do a thing to him, but he's always given me shit about the littlest things. He's a friend of Dad's, so I figured it had to do with that."

Holding open the door to the diner, he let his other hand touch Les' ass with a quick pat. Those brown eyes shot a wink at him and he chuckled. Les waved to a small, red-haired woman behind the counter as they sat down in a back booth. Slouching down on his side of the booth, he let his knee brush against Les'. A black eyebrow shot up at his audacity.

"Be careful, baby. You don't want me to give these innocent people a show," Les warned in a low voice.

He grinned, but, before he could reply, Sally came to the table.

"Hey there, cowboy. It's about time you stopped by. Tammy told me you were back a week ago. I thought you'd have stopped by before now." Sally shot Les a look then winked at Randy. "I guess you found more interesting things to do with your time."

He felt his face heat up. "Got stomped by a bronc couple of months ago. I decided to try and recover at the ranch. Didn't work out, but Les here was willing to give me a room at his place."

"Your daddy's a mean S.O.B. Thank goodness, Les is a much nicer man, though I hear you gave Skinner a little talking to today." Sally nodded at Les.

"A man can stand only so much incompetence before he breaks," Les said while studying the menu.

"True. So what will you boys have today?" She pulled out her order pad.

"It might still be morning, but I want some of your apple pie, Sally." Randy didn't even check the menu. He'd spent a lot of time at Sally's while he was in high school, trying to flirt with girls and fighting to ignore his attraction to his male classmates.

After Sally went to place their order, Les bumped his knee and smirked.

"Peter was checking you out, cowboy," the man teased.

"No, he wasn't," he denied while ducking his head to hide his smile.

"Yes, he was, and, if I hadn't let him know you were mine, I'm sure he'd have asked you out."

He studied Les but he didn't seem upset by Peter's flirting. "I wish I'd known Peter was gay back in high school. I might not have felt like such a freak."

"More than likely, you both would have been teased and tormented. It wouldn't have lasted very long."

Sally brought them their coffee and pie. Randy thought about Les' comment while Sally was at the table. The man was right. It wouldn't have lasted long because of the pressure they would have been under to conform. He would have left at eighteen no matter what. His dad's dislike of him didn't have anything to do with him being gay, though that was the fault his dad commented on the most.

"From a young age, I remember my dad getting mad at me about the strangest things. I couldn't understand why he hated me so much. Then, as I got older, I realised it wasn't just me he hated. He didn't like Tammy either. There was just something about his younger children he couldn't stand," Randy mused out loud before taking a bite of his pie.

"Younger children?" Les' voice held surprise.

"We have an older brother. I was only three when he left. Damn, Rick had to have been sixteen when he headed out on his own. I have no idea where he went, or if he's even alive anymore." Randy thought about his older brother for a moment. He felt a sudden longing to find him.

"Do you think your father was taking out his anger over Rick's leaving on you?" Les traced a pattern on the table.

"You could be right. I don't remember what the relationship between them was like. I was too young to be affected by it. My mom died when I was ten and I think that's when I realised that my dad didn't like anyone. He'd whip me for the smallest infraction, but he never touched Tammy. When I turned eighteen, I had enough. I would have taken Tammy with me, but she was only thirteen. I guess I knew he wouldn't hit her. I stay in touch with her and come back to the ranch on rare occasions." He smiled at Les. "Now that I know you're around here, I'll be coming back more often."

Les nudged his knee again. "There'll be a bed waiting for you when you do come home."

Blushing, he knew Les was talking about his own bed, not the guest one. "I just might take you up on that offer."

Les stood. "Let's head back to the ranch. We both have things to do today."

Thinking about what he had planned for them later on that night made him hard and he wasn't sure he wanted to walk out of the diner sporting an erection. He squirmed in his seat. Les looked down at him and the knowing look in the man's eyes told Randy that Les realised what his predicament was.

Licking his lips, Les gave him an evil little grin. "See what you've started, baby. Now you'll have to pay." Les started walking away. Randy sat and watched that jean-covered ass move. When Les figured out Randy wasn't with him, he turned and said, "Are you coming?"

"Unfortunately, no," Randy mumbled, leaping to his feet and rushing out of the diner. "I have to stop at the drug store for a moment. I'll meet you at the truck."

"Fine," Les called after him.

* * * *

Walking up to the cash register, Randy thought about how embarrassing this whole experience was. Buying lube and condoms at a store he'd shopped in since he was a kid had to be the dumbest idea he'd ever had. He dumped his items on the counter and looked up. Linda, one of his mother's best friends, was working the register. *Shit,* he thought.

"Hey, Randy, good to see you back." She didn't blink as she rang up the condoms. "How have you been? Rodeo treating you good?"

How was he supposed to have a normal conversation with her? Especially while she held the box of condoms he was planning on using to fuck another guy. "I've been pretty good, Linda. I'm in second place in the bareback standings. Got a little beat up, so I took some time off to heal up. I plan on riding at the Kaycee rodeo next month."

"Oh good. John and I'll come out to cheer you on." She bagged up his stuff and handed it to him with smile. "I hope you decide to settle down soon, Randy. Your mom wouldn't want you living like a vagabond."

"Considering who I'd be settling down with, I'm not sure she'd be too happy," he muttered as he turned to go.

Linda rested her hand on his arm. "She would have loved you anyway. I was her best friend and I know nothing you did would have changed her mind about that." She nodded out of the window to where Les waited in the truck. "Your ride's waiting for you. Try and be happy, Randy. That's the only thing she really wanted for you."

He slammed the truck door after sliding in. Sitting there for a moment, he thought about what Linda had said.

"You get what you needed?" Les asked, starting the truck.

"Yeah. Hey, can we stop by the flower shop and then head out to the cemetery?" It had been a year since he had visited his mother's grave.

"Sure," Les agreed, but didn't ask why.

* * * *

Les stood back, watching Randy make his way to the graveside. His lover held a bouquet of daisies in a trembling hand. Les wondered what had made Randy decide to visit his mother's grave, but hadn't objected when the man had asked to go. The cowboy turned and gestured for Les to join him.

When he reached Randy, he slipped his arm around the lean waist and moved to block some of the wind. Randy rested his head on Les' shoulder.

"I wish you could have met her." A hint of sadness touched Randy's voice.

"I bet she was pretty," Les commented.

"Why?" Randy moved away to kneel and trace the letters on the stone.

"As good-looking as you and your sister are, I know it didn't come from your father," Les teased.

"I don't remember what she looked like. All I really remember is her laughter. The sun seemed to shine a little brighter when she was happy." Randy peeked up at him.

Les could tell he was embarrassed. Kneeling next to him, he tipped Randy's brown cowboy hat back on the dark curls and brushed a kiss over a flushed cheek. "That's a great memory to have. I wish I knew my mother. Dad did his best to give me some idea of what she was like. He showed me tons of pictures and always talked about her, but I never had a real memory like you."

"Do you still have those pictures?" Randy cleared a spot at the base of the stone and laid the bouquet there.

"Yes, they're boxed up with several photo albums my dad kept." He hugged Randy tight to him for a second. Standing, he held out his hand to help him up. "Why don't we go home and after dinner we can look at them?"

"Okay." Randy took Les' hand and allowed him to pull him to his feet.

Chapter Thirteen

Les came in from feeding the horses to find the dinner table set with the nice china and silver. It was an intimate setting with the plates at one end of the table. Sniffing the air, he went into the kitchen. Margie was bustling between the stove and counter.

"What's the occasion?" he asked after kissing her.

"You need to go and clean up. I don't want Master Randy's plans screwed up." Margie pushed him towards his bedroom.

"Randy's plans?" He looked back at her.

"This morning he asked me to cook your favourite dinner. Which I might add is almost ready." Margie shooed him away. "Master Randy came in a few minutes ago. Go take a shower."

He didn't want to put a name to the emotion tugging at his heart. It made him feel good to know Randy wanted to have a special night with him. He had a feeling he knew what was going to happen later on. After tugging off his clothes, he headed to the bathroom.

The steam fogged the room when he'd turned on the shower. He avoided looking at his reflection in the mirror. There had been a time when he'd have checked to make sure there were no blemishes, just like a teenage girl, but no more. The dent and scar on his head, along with the surgery scars, made him cringe. No longer was he perfect, and that was why Taylor had left him.

Stepping under the hot water, he allowed his memories to wash away. Taylor was part of his past. While he would never forget the man or the hurt, he wouldn't dwell on them. It was way past time to love again and if he were lucky enough to find a man he could love forever, he'd consider all his pain worth it. As he scrubbed the sweat and dirt off his body, he thought about the past week.

For the first time in years, he was enjoying getting up in the morning. He had found something to smile about during the day. Spending time with Randy was slowly freeing him from the burden of his injuries. He had watched Randy spread his wings and come out of the darkness. Being in the closet wasn't terrible and for some people it was safer for them to stay there. If Randy showed any hesitation about coming out, Les wouldn't push. He had the feeling that Randy had just been looking for support to take that last step, though. Les vowed to be there for the cowboy, even if the relationship didn't get any deeper than it was at the moment.

After jumping out of the shower, he dried off and hurried into his bedroom. He searched through his closet for his favourite dress shirt. Its brilliant blue colour matched Randy's eyes and its soft cotton material comforted him. He pulled on a pair of jeans, but didn't worry about socks or shoes. Padding back down to the living room, he walked in to find Randy pacing.

His breath caught in his throat. Dark brown curls glistened in the low lamplight, proving that Randy had taken a shower as well. The black jeans Randy wore hugged his lean hips and showed the bulge behind the zipper off to perfection. Les felt his own jeans start to become uncomfortably tight. The tan Western-style shirt covered broad shoulders and the snaps taunted Les to come and rip them open. He must have made some noise because Randy stopped and turned to look at him.

They came together with a thud. He filled his hands with tight cowboy butt and Randy cupped the back of his head. Les didn't flinch like he normally did when anyone got close to the depression in his skull. He focused his mind on Randy's mouth.

He took Randy without hesitation. His tongue gained entrance and duelled with Randy's. He sucked in the full bottom lip and nibbled on it. Groaning, Randy rubbed against him.

"Wrap your leg around my thigh," he murmured, trailing kisses over Randy's chin and down his neck.

One long leg entwined around his own, causing their groins to meet and rub against each other. He lifted Randy so he was standing on the tip of his toes for a different angle, and started rocking his hips. Randy's head fell back, giving him better access to the tender spot right beneath the ear. He tasted it with his teeth and sucked. A need to mark the man built in him, but he wouldn't do it until he knew for sure Randy was totally out of the closet.

"Les," Randy groaned. His voice was hoarse with passion.

"Hmm...you taste good," he whispered, making his way down to where the tendon connecting the neck and shoulder rested. A hard bite made Randy jerk.

"I want..." Randy's passion seemed to be short-circuiting his brain.

A noise came from the dining room. Randy must have remembered Margie and dinner at the same moment Les did, from the way Randy froze. Les let go of Randy's ass and set the man back down on his feet.

"Master Leslie and Master Randy, dinner is ready," Margie called from the other room.

Les figured she had seen them kissing, which was why she hadn't come in to tell them face-to-face. He stepped away from Randy, but ran his thumb over his kiss-swollen lips. "Let's enjoy the dinner Margie made and then we'll enjoy each other."

Randy nodded and led the way to the table. Les saw their glasses held iced tea. He glanced at the dark-haired man. "You can have a beer, Randy. Just because I can't drink doesn't mean you can't."

"It's okay. I don't really like beer anyway. It's easier to order that than to ask for a soda in a bar."

Les ran his foot up Randy's calf and smiled as he jerked. "Thank you for asking Margie to make my favourites."

Shrugging, Randy smiled shyly at him. "I thought you might like something special tonight."

Leering at him, Les winked. "I think I'm going to get something very special later on."

"Eat," Randy choked out while trying not to laugh.

* * * *

The last plate was set in the sink and Randy felt the butterflies in his stomach start dancing again. How could he have thought he'd actually be able to go through with it? Les was used to men who were far more experienced than Randy was. *He seemed to enjoy the things you've done so far,* a voice sounded in his mind.

Arms wrapped around his waist and he leant back on Les. Warm breath caressed his ear as Les asked, "What are you thinking about?"

"I'm starting to panic a little," he admitted.

"Panic? Why?" Les turned him around and rested his hands on Randy's hips.

"I've been thinking about all the stuff you must have done and how I haven't done any of it." He sounded pathetic.

"I am eight years older than you, Randy. I've had more time to do things. Also, I've never had to keep my sexual preferences a secret. I'd think that'd put a damper on any kind of relationship. I haven't complained yet, have I?" Les' brown eyes were earnest.

"Damn, I sound like a sixteen-year-old virgin," he muttered. Les' chuckle had him frowning at the man.

"You wouldn't be here if you were sixteen, baby." Warm lips brushed his cheeks. "Would you feel better if we looked at my family pictures? We don't need to rush this."

He didn't know what to say. He wanted to take the next step in their relationship. The pressure was building. It was as if, once he'd made the decision to have real sex with Les, he didn't want to wait, but he didn't know what to do.

"Go and sit out on my patio, baby. I'll be there in a moment." Les kissed him softly then turned him towards the bedroom.

He went. *So much for taking charge of the seduction,* he thought as he settled into the lounge chair under the Wyoming night sky. Staring up at the stars, he found himself wishing on one for the courage to make a commitment to Les for as long as the ride lasted.

"Are you wishing on the stars?" Les' voice came from the darkened bedroom.

Les moved into the moonlight. He'd stripped down to a pair of boxer-briefs and he was holding a bowl. Randy scooted over to let Les join him on the chair.

"We forgot to have dessert." Les held out the bowl and Randy realised it was full of strawberry shortcake covered in whipped cream. "I adore strawberries and Margie's shortcake is to die for."

"I'm partial to chocolate cake myself." Randy cleared his throat.

"We'll have to let Margie know. She loves baking." Les scooped up a spoonful of strawberries and held it out for Randy to eat. Before he could take the bite, Les pulled it back and said, "You should take your clothes off. It might get messy."

Standing up, Randy felt a little foolish, stripping outside where anyone could see him. He just hoped the ranch hands were either in the bunkhouse or busy somewhere else on the ranch. He let his shirt fall to the ground where it was then joined by his jeans. Hooking his fingers in the waistband of his briefs, he gave Les a questioning look. Les nodded and he tugged his underwear off.

"That's better. Now come over here." Les gestured for him to stand in front of him.

Randy was glad Les seemed to be taking charge. It wasn't that he didn't want to direct their lovemaking, but he wasn't sure what to do. He gasped as something wet and cool landed on his cock. Looking down, he watched in surprise as Les scooped another spoonful of strawberries and cream onto his heated flesh.

Les' dark gaze gleamed up at him. "I want to lick the cream off your cock."

Okay, so it wasn't very manly, but he swore his knees buckled at Les' statement. He reached out and supported his body on Les' shoulders. "I'm not going to stop you," he managed to say.

"Good." Les leant forward and swiped his tongue along the underside of Randy's shaft.

Randy's eyes rolled back in his head and he couldn't stop the full-body shudder from overtaking him. The coolness of the cream combined with the heat of Les' tongue shot desire through him. Another long lick caused a groan to escape.

"Les," he cried out softly as Les swallowed down to the base of his cock.

The suction Les created with his mouth caused the man's cheeks to hollow out. Randy caressed the stubble-rough depressions. Even in the lessening light, he could see how beautiful Les looked while sucking on him. The man pulled off him with a pop.

"No," he protested, not wanting to lose the almost overwhelming sensations.

"Shh, baby. It's okay. Come with me." Les took him by the hand and led him back into the dark bedroom. "Spread out on your back." Les pointed at the bed.

Les must have pulled the blankets down before he came out to the patio. Towels were arranged over the sheets and Randy lay on his back. Les was standing next to the bed, shaking a can. As he watched, Les squirted some more whipped cream onto his finger and licked it off.

"I love cream. Margie makes sure there's always a can or two in the fridge for me. Maybe I should tell her to buy a bigger supply, because I think I'm going to be developing a taste for licking it off your cock."

Randy's hips jerked and he arched off the bed, silently begging for Les' touch. The sound of the can mixed with the first silken touch of the cream made him jump. He looked down, watching Les coat his cock with cream, making it into one large mound of white. A laugh burst from him.

"What are you laughing at, baby?" Les looked up at him with an innocent expression on his face.

"I can't help but wonder, what is sexy about my dick being decorated like an ice cream sundae?" He chuckled again.

Les dropped a strawberry slice on the top of the cream mountain. They watched it start to slide down. "Better get that before it spills off," Les murmured and bent forward.

Randy let his head fall back against the pillows and closed his eyes. A deep moan came from him as Les started to feast on his shaft. Light little flicks of a tip. Long hard swipes from the flat of the tongue. Nips from teeth to keep him guessing. Soon he was awash in sensations. While Les' mouth worked his cock mercilessly, the man's hands stroked his hips and thighs. Calloused fingers fondled his balls and slipped back to tease his hole. His thighs were sprawled open and he didn't care how wanton he looked, he just wanted Les to continue what he was doing.

His neck began to tingle and passion built at the base of his spine. Randy's balls tightened and all he could do was grunt a warning to Les that he was about to come. Les didn't stop sucking him. The man swallowed him down and, when the head of his shaft hit the back of Les' throat, he came long and hard.

"Shit," he breathed when the last of his spasms had died. He ran a limp hand over Les' head, thanking him with silent touches.

"Did you enjoy that?" Les moved away from him, still caressing his trembling thighs.

"I'm never going to be able to look at another can of whipped cream without getting a hard-on," he joked.

"Good." Les looked around the room. "Where did you put the condoms and lube you bought earlier today?"

He'd be embarrassed if he had the energy. "In the nightstand." He pointed to the one on the right hand side.

"Stay right there," Les ordered as he stood up to retrieve the items.

Randy's gaze went to the long, curved cock bobbing between Les' thighs. The head rose to brush the ridged stomach above it, leaving a wet trail behind. A hint of apprehension tried to sneak in. As much as he wanted Les to fuck him, he wasn't sure how it was going to work. Les dropped the lube and rubbers on the bed then stretched out beside him.

"It was probably silly to get condoms since I've never done it before and you're clean." He felt foolish now.

Les shook his head. "It's not foolish, Randy. Always play it safe. Never ever take anyone's word about something like this. We'll use rubbers for a while. If we're heading for a long-term relationship, we'll go get tested."

Randy's heart skipped a beat at the thought of a long-term relationship with Les. Riding the rodeo would put pressure on both of them, especially if he chose not to be out on the circuit. He must have been frowning, because Les ran a finger between his eyebrows.

"Don't worry about it tonight, Randy. We've got time to learn each other and see if we'll fit together." Les leant down and kissed him.

Chapter Fourteen

A mixture of sweet and salt greeted Randy's tongue as he swept it into Les' mouth. Whipped cream flavoured with his own essence. He sighed as Les' lube-slicked hand pumped his shaft.

"I don't think I'll be getting it up again for a while," he whispered against Les' lips.

Warm breath burst over his mouth when Les chuckled. "Don't worry, baby. I'm just keeping you interested and relaxed. Trust me. You'll come again before I'm done."

He wanted to say he'd trust Les with his life, but he didn't think it was time for declarations like that. Letting go of his worries, he slid his hands around Les' waist and held on. His thighs were spread farther apart as Les' fingers skimmed over the smooth skin behind his balls. He never imagined a touch there could make him restless, but he shifted slightly against the towels under his back.

"Oh," he gasped as Les pressed a finger against his opening.

"Try and relax," Les suggested, pulling the finger away and adding more lube. "It'd be easier if you were on your hands and knees, but I want to watch your face while I take you."

He cradled Les' face in his hand and smiled. "Since you'll be my first, I want to be able to memorise your face."

Les kissed him then moved to kneel between his legs. "Pull your legs up."

Randy brought them up to his chest and spread them open, exposing all of his body to Les' gaze. Passion glazed the man's brown eyes for a moment.

"Beautiful," Les murmured, running a finger from the tip of Randy's cock to his hole.

He wanted to say that men weren't beautiful, but he couldn't get the words to form. Les was pressing a finger into him and to his virgin ass it felt like a tree limb. He was distracted from the pressure by Les leaning down and swallowing his cock again. Randy moved with small thrusts, rocking between the warm, wet mouth and the slick finger. At one point, Les twisted his finger and nailed something inside Randy. He froze when a shot of electricity seemed to jolt through him.

"Again," he grunted, speeding up his own motions. Soon he was fucking himself on Les' hand while Les feasted on his erection. His lover managed to bump that same point each time.

After a few minutes, Les pulled away from him. "You're going to get two now," Les warned him. He took a deep breath and nodded.

"Shit," he swore as Les pressed his fingers and a slight pinch of pain tensed his muscles.

"Breathe, baby," Les instructed before he took Randy's shaft back in his mouth.

Les' free hand touched him everywhere. His chest, nipples, stomach and balls were caressed while Les stretched him. Lust swamped him and he rode the waves, trying to climb his pleasure to a climax. So caught up in passion, he didn't notice when Les took his fingers out and started to push his own cock in. A few inches in and he flinched. Les stopped.

"Tell me when I can move again," Les told him.

Randy had the feeling he wouldn't have got such consideration if he had chosen some cowboy on the circuit to be his first. 'In and out.' 'Come and leave.' Those were the mottos gays lived by in the rodeo. He tried to force his body to relax, but it wasn't until Les leant forward and kissed him that he felt comfortable. His body opened and it seemed like he pulled Les' cock deep into him.

"Les." He couldn't think. His brain was fried and all he could do was feel. Les rode him slow at first, like he was a young horse being broken to saddle and rider for the first time. Randy started to push back and move with the man, encouraging him to take him harder.

The smell of sex and sweat filled the air. Randy reached down and started to stroke his cock to the tempo of Les' thrusts. His balls tightened and he groaned.

"Coming," he told Les.

"Want to feel you come on my cock." Les' voice was harsh and demanding.

Randy pumped his cock once more and flicked a thumbnail over the weeping slit. His climax ripped through him and ropes of pearly cum coated his hand and stomach. His ass clamped down on Les' cock. Les threw his head back and cried out as Randy milked his shaft until there was nothing left.

When Les pulled out, Randy winced. He was going to be sore tomorrow, but he figured it was a good pain. Randy stared up at the ceiling while Les went into the bathroom. He stretched, having never felt such an ache before. Yet, for all the discomfort he might have to deal with, he wasn't unhappy about letting Les fuck him. *Maybe this will be the start of something special. Something far different than I've ever encountered.*

Les came back, holding a damp towel, and Randy let the man clean him off. After taking all of the towels back to the other room, Les climbed back into bed and spooned behind Randy. Running his hand over the hair on Les' arm, Randy thought about what had happened. His fingers touched a jagged scar running around Les' thumb.

"What's this from?" He traced it.

Les' breath warmed the back of his neck. "I got it tangled up in some reins and the horse reared. Almost took the thumb off."

"Rough. I injured my wrist that way." He grimaced, remembering the pain.

"Yeah, it was, but I learnt not to wrap the reins around my hand like that again." Les stroked a hand down the middle of Randy's chest. "Are you okay?"

"Yeah." He lifted his shoulder slightly. "Just thinking."

"Hmm." Les kissed his back.

He stayed silent and Les didn't push him. Randy was glad because he didn't know how to explain his feelings. His instincts were telling him that Les was quickly becoming very important to him. He wanted to believe it was just a crush, or the wild, turbulent feelings anyone had for the person they gave their virginity to, but those same instincts weren't buying it.

Tonight was the start of something he could see lasting forever. Les' even breathing brushed his skin and he found himself filling his lungs in the same rhythm. He shifted restlessly, his thoughts not allowing him to sleep.

Les tugged him tighter, letting Randy rest his head on an arm while placing his own hand on Randy's stomach. "Give it up, baby. Think about all this shit tomorrow morning."

Sighing, Randy melted back into the warm body behind him. He'd take the man's advice. Maybe tomorrow would bring answers. He closed his eyes and slipped into dreams of riding across the Wyoming plains with Les beside him.

* * * *

Les stared down at the man sprawled across his bed. He'd woken up and used the bathroom. Since he was up, he decided to put the whipped cream back in the fridge. By the time he'd got back to the room, Randy had rolled over on his stomach and taken over most of the mattress. He patted the bare bubble butt once and moved towards the doors he'd forgotten to close.

Wrapping the blanket he'd grabbed from the couch around him, he settled in the chair. He stared up into the star-strewn sky and thought about the day. The ranch was doing well. No problem with the bills and he was thinking about expanding the breeding stock. He'd have to talk to Jackson about it, and maybe ask Randy for some advice. Randy had good ideas and Les wasn't above taking advantage of that.

His anger tried to escape when he thought about the episode in the feed store. He pushed his emotions away. No reason to get all excited about that again.

He'd rectified the situation and it wouldn't happen again. He might have got a bookkeeper for the ranch as well, if Peter decided to take him up on his offer. Though, on second thoughts, maybe he didn't want the good-looking young man around. Randy's eyes might be drawn away from his beat-up old body for some fresher meat.

Stop feeling sorry for yourself. He grinned. Every time he'd started whining about the accident and his injuries, his father had told him that other people were worse off. The man had been right. At least Les could walk and talk again. He might not be able to ride competitively, but he could still ride. Maybe he'd lost the only man he'd thought he'd ever love but he'd found strength and a certain freedom in not living in Taylor's shadow anymore.

A noise came from the bedroom and he smiled. Since his accident, he'd learnt that life was funny. Moments that seemed like the end of the world were really only the beginning steps to whole new journeys, and this new one might be the best of his life.

A coyote howled his lone cry into the night air. One of the horses nickered in the barns. A cow lowed softly in the distant darkness. He rested his head on the back of the chair and closed his eyes. These night sounds were different from the ones he'd grown up with in Virginia, but he'd got used to them over time and they'd become the lullaby he fell asleep to now. He let the noises ease his thoughts and relax his body.

A car door slammed in front of the house and he came to his feet. Making his way through the bedroom, he grabbed a pair of jeans and a shirt. He stopped long enough to tug the pants on and zip them up but he didn't bother to button them. Slipping the T-shirt on, he headed for the front door.

He opened the door to find Jackson about to knock. Tammy stood behind him, her arm wrapped around the shoulders of a young woman. He felt a hand touch his back and knew Randy stood behind him. Stepping back, he gestured for the trio to come in.

"Randy, can you go and start a pot of coffee?" he asked his lover.

Randy nodded and went to the kitchen. Les led the way to the living room. Tammy sat down next to the woman on the couch. Jackson stood behind them with his hand on Tammy's shoulder. Les didn't say anything until after the coffee was ready and everyone had a cup.

"So what's going on?" he asked when Randy sat down on the arm of the chair he was sitting in.

"We were wondering if Lindsay could stay here for a day or two, boss," Jackson spoke first.

"Lindsay," Randy murmured. Standing up, his cowboy went to kneel in front of the woman. "Lindsay Macintosh?"

The woman lifted her head and tired green eyes met Randy's. "Hey, Randy." Her voice was weak.

Les studied her trembling hands—she could hardly hold the coffee cup. He caught Tammy's eyes and nodded towards the mug. Randy's sister took the coffee and set it down on the end table.

"What the hell happened to you?" Randy touched the woman's rail-thin arm.

"Lindsay's sick, Randy. She just needs somewhere to recuperate for a while," Tammy interjected.

Lindsay shot the woman a glance. "Tell them the truth, Tammy. If they're going to take me in, they need to know what they're going to be getting into."

Les crossed his legs and settled back into the chair. "Am I going to need to hire extra men, Jackson?"

"No, sir. There's no one after her."

"Tell me."

Les smiled at the soft order in Randy's voice. Lindsay was skittish, but it didn't come from abuse. Les had seen victims of domestic violence before and they wouldn't have been able to be in the same room with three men.

"I took a wrong turn after high school, I guess. I went to New York. Thought I'd get a modelling contract. Well, what I got was addicted and almost lost my life. I overdosed but didn't manage to kill myself. After I got out of the hospital, I told myself I wouldn't do coke anymore. It seems addictions are harder to break than I thought." A rueful smile graced her lips.

Les could see the beauty hidden in the skeletal face. With more weight and sleep, Lindsay would be gorgeous. Cocaine had a habit of stripping everything from a person. The white powder took their youth, their pride and their lives. Les had seen what the use of the drug could do while he rode the show circuit.

"Addiction to anything is bad and terribly difficult to stop," he agreed with her. After his accident, he'd taken so many painkillers that, if his father hadn't stepped in when he had, Les would have been an addict for the rest of his life. "Why come to my house? You must have family in the area."

"When I left for New York, my parents threw a fit. They expected me to stay around, get married and raise a brood of children, just like they did. I wanted something more. They haven't got over it yet. After my second overdose, I decided to come back here. Maybe it would help. I called my sister. She couldn't go against family, but she asked Tammy to pick me up at the airport." Lindsay flashed Tammy a grateful smile.

"We picked her up, but she doesn't have anywhere to stay. Daddy would never allow her to stay at our place." Tammy stared at him with pleading eyes.

"Exactly what type of reputation will she have when the townsfolk learn she's living with a gay man?" Les figured he'd get that out in the open.

Randy stood up and came over to him. Winking at him, Randy smiled and said, "Two gay men. At least until I start riding the circuit again."

Lindsay didn't look shocked. She shrugged. "I've got a bad reputation already. Living with you won't make it worse. I've got through the worst of detox. Now I'm looking for some peace and quiet. I need to regain my strength and figure out where the hell I'm going now."

Les looked up at Randy, silently asking him his opinion. Randy nodded.

"You can stay here for as long as you need. When you feel up to it, maybe you can help Margie around the house. It should keep you from getting bored." He stood and held out a hand to her. "I'm Les Hardin, by the way."

"Lindsay Macintosh. Les Hardin, huh? Didn't you used to ride horses out east?" A frown formed between her eyebrows as she tried to place him.

"Yes, I did. I retired about six years ago and came out to try something new."

"Now I remember. Your partner used to be that absolutely to-die-for gorgeous Taylor Lourdin. My friends were so jealous of you." She slapped a hand over her mouth as Randy moved to his side. "Oh, I'm sorry."

"Yes, Taylor was my partner, but that was a long time ago." For the first time, the memory of Taylor didn't hurt and Les knew it had something to do with the man standing next to him. Randy slid an arm around his waist and he leaned into his hard body. He felt a twinge in his left arm. It was time to go back to bed. "Jackson, get Lindsay settled in the other guest room. Don't forget to leave a note to warn Margie we have a new visitor."

Moving back towards their bedroom, he let Randy support some of his weight. His lover didn't say anything until they were in bed and wrapped around each other.

"Are you okay?" Randy's hand traced lines down his spine.

"I'm fine. Just tired. Got more exercise than normal tonight. My arm hurts a little." Les pressed a kiss to Randy's chest. "No big deal."

Randy was quiet and he knew the man was thinking about something.

"Ask me, baby."

"Do you miss him?" The question was asked in a casual voice, but Les knew Randy was deeply interested in his answer.

He took a moment to think about what he would say. "For a long time after the accident, I did miss him. I was hurt and had lost the one thing I loved more than anything else in the world and then he walked out on me. It crushed me. He was telling me that I wasn't worth anything anymore because I was broken. There were days my dad had to work hard to get me to even try and get better." He remembered how frustrated his father would get with him.

"What turned you around?"

He didn't move away when Randy reached up and ran light fingers over the dent in his skull. Pushing his body up, he settled against the headboard and grabbed the picture on the nightstand. "Here's what turned me around." He showed it to Randy. "My dad told me what Sam did for me. I realised if I didn't get better and learn to ride again, then Taylor would find a way to get rid of Sam. There was no way I was going to let that horse get sold or be destroyed because I was too much of a coward to help him. I told Dad to sell the stable to Taylor, but to make sure Sam wasn't part of the deal. Dad helped me find this place, but he never saw me ride again. He died before I left the hospital."

Randy rested his head on Les' lap and stared up at him. Smiling down at the dark-haired man, Les rubbed his thumb over Randy's cheek.

"I wish I could have met him. Your dad sounds like a wonderful man." Randy's face held a wistful expression and Les figured the cowboy was thinking about his own dad.

"I think he would have liked you. He wasn't very impressed with Taylor, but he dealt with him because of me." Les set the picture back down and laid his hand on Randy's chest, over the spot where his heart was beating. "Tonight, when Lindsay mentioned Taylor, I realised something."

"What was that?" Randy's hand covered his and entwined their fingers.

"It didn't hurt. I've probably been over Taylor for a while now. It's just my feelings for him were tangled up with my emotions at not being able to ride competitively anymore." A tremor racked his left arm. Closing his eyes, he waited for it to stop.

"What did you like about competing?" Randy pressed a kiss right above his belly button.

"The connection between me and the horse. It was almost as if Sam would read my mind. The thrill of clearing six foot fences without touching them and doing it at the fastest pace we could. The sounds and sights of the shows. There's an excitement that's almost electric at a horse show, especially where the top horses and riders are competing. I've never felt happier than when I was out in the ring, staring at huge jumps and knowing that, without a screw-up from me, Sam would jump all of them clean."

Randy laughed. "Your eyes light up when you talk about it. I know what you mean though. There's that same excitement at rodeos. I'd like to see a Grand Prix."

"Maybe when you can take some time off from the circuit, we'll fly out east to the Hamptons and hit the show there. It's one of the biggest shows of the outdoor season. You'll be able to see the best horses and riders there." He knew Taylor would probably be there as well, but seeing his ex-lover again wouldn't bother him, especially if Randy was there.

His head hurt just enough that he knew he should take something for it. Sighing, he climbed out of bed.

"Where are you going?" Randy sat up, tucking the blankets around his lean hips.

"I've got to get something for my headache. If I don't, I won't be able to sleep." He rummaged around in the bathroom cabinet. After finding what he needed, he swallowed the pills with some water and rejoined Randy in bed.

Les let Randy wiggle around until Randy held him tight to his chest. He rested his head on a broad shoulder and let his medicine carry him into sleep.

Chapter Fifteen

Swimming up out of the fog of sleep, Les heard the sound of singing. He rolled over on his back and glanced at the clock. It was almost ten in the morning. The medicine had really knocked him out. He stared up at the ceiling, trying to clear his mind enough to figure out where the singing was coming from.

The bathroom door opened and Randy walked out. Except for drying his hair with a towel, the man was naked. Les gave a wolf whistle. Randy blushed but, dropping the towel, he climbed onto the mattress. On his hands and knees, Randy crawled up Les' body until their lips touched. Mint played on his tongue when he thrust it into Randy's mouth. He nibbled on the full bottom lip and along the strong jaw. He ran his tongue down the skin Randy offered to him. Blowing to dry the line, he saw a shiver run over the lean body.

"I want skin," Randy ordered.

Les didn't argue. They managed to push the blankets aside without losing touch with each other. He cupped Randy's ass and pulled the man down so their chests were tight together. Moving slightly, he arranged their positions so Randy's cock rested against his.

"Feels good," Randy mumbled as the cowboy started rubbing on Les.

"Yes, it does," Les agreed, enjoying the sensation of hard muscles and warm skin surrounding him.

They rocked together gently while they memorised sensitive spots to make the other man gasp. They found tender places, causing moans to fill the morning air. Passion built slowly as Les learnt what turned his new lover on. Apparently everything did, because each of Les' touches made Randy writhe and whimper. Randy's tempo began to stutter as Les' fingers skimmed over the area above his crease then down to tease his hole.

Wet heat splashed between their bodies and Randy cried out softly. Les came almost at the same time. Not caring about being sticky, Les gathered the other man close and sighed.

"Good morning, baby." He kissed Randy's cheek.

Randy murmured something, but, with his face buried in Les' chest, his words were indistinguishable. After a few minutes, Randy pushed his upper body off Les and grinned down at him.

"I guess I'm going to need another shower," he teased.

Les smiled. "I could use some company while I take mine."

"Deal." Randy jumped to his feet and pulled Les to his.

"To be young again," Les joked as he was tugged towards the bathroom. "Or do you just want to get me wet and slick?"

Suddenly the image of him bent over in the shower with Randy fucking his ass burst into his mind and he groaned. Randy looked back at him from where he was turning the water on.

"You okay?" Randy gripped his shoulder.

"Maybe we make this a first time shower," he managed to say around his thick tongue.

"A first time shower? We've taken showers together before." Randy looked puzzled.

"There's something you haven't done yet." Reaching in the drawer under the sink, Les pulled out a condom and lube.

"That's true. I haven't been fucked in the shower yet." A wide grin spread across Randy's face.

Les could see how much that thought turned Randy on by the way his long, curved cock filled again. Shaking his head, Les stroked a finger up the underside of Randy's shaft.

"I'm the one who's going to get fucked in the shower. You interested in topping?"

Randy pushed him into the shower, plastering that lean body against him, and he laughed.

"I take that to mean yes."

"I don't know what to do. I don't want to hurt you." Randy ran his hands over Les' body, tweaking nipples and stroking Les' erection.

"You won't hurt me, baby. Just make sure I'm ready for you and have fun." Les drew the man's face up for a kiss and handed the lube to his lover. "Use the lube."

Turning, he braced his hands on the tiles of the shower stall and tilted his hips.

"Oh," Randy breathed against his neck as the man pressed his chest to Les' back.

Rubbing his ass on Randy, Les felt the warmer moisture coming from the flared head of his lover's cock. He arched his back when a rough hand trailed down his spine to dip into his crease. It had been a long time since he'd bottomed, so he was prepared for a little pain. He pushed back at the first tentative touch of a fingertip at his hole. They both gasped as the finger breached the first ring of muscle.

Randy's forehead came to rest between Les' shoulder blades and Les could feel Randy's lips moving against his skin. The pounding water made it impossible to hear what the cowboy was saying. He moved slightly and Randy's finger slid farther in.

"Baby, you can move," he instructed, throwing the words over his shoulder.

A shudder rippled through his body as Randy bumped his knuckle against Les' gland. The man must have noticed because he ran his finger over it again. Les leaned his head against the wall and began to rock with the thrusts. Soon the head of his cock was bumping the wall in front of him.

"Should I put two in now?" Randy asked.

With all the sensations swirling in him, he could only grunt and hope Randy took that as a yes. The burning he felt with the next twist of Randy's fingers told him Randy understood. He spread his thighs and bent over more, making sure that Randy's fingers hit his gland every time. Randy must have been paying attention when Les had prepared him last night. A third finger slid in and he moaned.

Randy moved to his side and wrapped his free hand around Les' cock. Les thrust his hips, fucking himself on Randy's fingers and relishing the tightness of the hot hand holding him. His balls drew up and a tingling built through his body.

"Gonna come, baby," he gasped.

"Wait." Randy gripped the base of Les' shaft like a vice.

Les dropped his head and breathed deep, trying to gain a little control over the pleasure threatening to erupt from him. Randy disappeared behind him. He heard the tear of the condom wrapper and, a minute later, the touch of the blunt head of Randy's cock at his opening.

"Take it slow. It's been a while for me." Les pushed back and sighed as Randy filled him, slowly but inevitably.

A light kiss brushed the nape of his neck. "Are you okay?" Randy asked. It sounded like he was fighting not to move.

"Yeah. Move, baby."

His permission unleashed Randy. The cowboy rode him hard and deep. His flared head bumped against his gland with each thrust, shooting electric shocks straight to his cock. Les fisted his own shaft and started pumping in time with Randy's reaming of his ass.

"Les," Randy called out and the hands on his hips bruised him with their grip.

"That's it. I'm going to come," he warned. His climax ripped through him and his cum splashed against the wall in front of him, covering his hands and stomach as well.

Les' inner muscles clamped down and massaged Randy's cock. Randy couldn't believe how warm and tight the man's passage was. Moving faster, his climax began to grow until he couldn't control it anymore.

"Shit," he moaned as he filled the condom—he had to lock his knees to keep from falling over. One last thrust and he collapsed against Les. His lover's arms shook from holding them both up. When they caught their breath, he pulled out and they cleaned up.

After drying off, Les smiled at him. He couldn't quite make his mind work. His climax seemed to have fried his brain. Les dried him off before leading him to the bed. He crawled under the blankets Les held up for him.

"I should be going to do something," he mumbled.

"A little snuggling is good. There's nothing that has to be done right away," Les suggested as his lover wrapped his arms around him and pulled him close.

"Maybe a little nap." His eyes closed while he talked.

Les brushed his lips over his forehead.

* * * *

An hour later, Les reached down and shook Randy gently. "Baby, it's time to get up."

Randy's sleepy eyes blinked open and a shy smile graced his face. "Hey, there."

"We better be making an appearance soon or they'll start to wonder what happened to us." Les stroked his hand over Randy's dark curls.

Randy's cheeks turned red, but the cowboy didn't leap out of bed as Les had expected. One of Randy's hands eased around Les' neck and the other around his waist. He allowed him to bring their lips together in a soft kiss. Randy pulled back and rubbed a thumb over his swollen bottom lip.

"Thank you," Randy whispered.

"For what, baby?" Les frowned.

"For being my first." Randy laughed. "I guess you're my first everything."

"At least you won't forget me." Les took Randy's hand and pulled the man out from under the covers. Taking him in his arms, he hugged him tight and said, "You're welcome."

They stood holding each other for a minute or two. A shout drifted in through the open window. Les chuckled. "What are you going to do for the rest of the morning?"

"I'll check on Folsom. Maybe see if he'll let me get a saddle on him. Then I'll go see Sally Jane and the colt. After that, how about you and I grab a picnic basket and go for a ride? I know a great spot for lunch," Randy suggested while he dressed.

"Sounds good. I have some paperwork to finish up before then." He pulled on some jeans and a shirt.

They exchanged another leisurely kiss before leaving the bedroom. Les patted Randy's tight ass when they parted ways in the hallway.

"I'll see you at lunch."

* * * *

Randy stood in the doorway of Les' office and watched the man work. He didn't think he'd ever get tired of looking at that handsome face and well-built body. There was a feeling of pride and awe in knowing Les wanted him as much as he wanted the other man. His cock filled out and his jeans grew tight. Reaching down, he tried to adjust himself for more comfort. His movement caught Les' attention.

Those brown eyes he'd thought were so sad when they'd first met lightened with a smile.

"Hey there, handsome. Done playing cowboy for a while?" Les waved him over to the desk.

He sauntered in, rolling his hips and drawing Les' gaze to the bulge in his jeans. "Maybe I just came in search of a different kind of ride." He flushed. He couldn't believe he was flirting with another man like this.

"I think a ride can be arranged." Les reached up and grabbed his wrist.

He let the other man pull him down so he was sitting on Les' lap. He cupped the back of Les' head and brought the man's mouth to his. Les opened to him when he swiped his tongue over his bottom lip. Their tongues duelled, playing and teasing each other. Changing the angle of his head, he made the kiss deeper and harder.

"Disgusting!" A shocked voice rang out through the room.

He broke away from Les and glanced over his shoulder to see Lindsay's younger sister standing in the office doorway. He stiffened and tried to climb off Les' lap, but his lover wouldn't allow him.

"Who the hell are you and what are you doing in my house?" Les' voice was cold.

Randy could tell the man was angry by the strength in the arms holding him.

"I'm Lindsay's sister, Anna. I can't believe you, Randy Hersch. You should be ashamed of yourself." The young woman's voice sliced into Randy.

He felt the insane urge to hide. Hers was the reaction he'd been afraid of.

"Why should he be ashamed?" Les glared at Anna.

"He's embarrassing his family by doing all this unnatural stuff." Anna grimaced as if she'd just tasted something rotten.

Randy found himself standing on his own feet and Les was advancing on Anna. The woman backpedalled as fast as she could, but Les took a hold of her arm. Randy followed as his lover dragged Anna down the hallway to the front door. Lindsay met them there. Opening the door, Les set the woman on the front porch.

"You can take any of the ranch vehicles you want to drive for visiting your sister. She is no longer welcome in my house," Les told Lindsay. He turned back to face Anna. "This is my house and what I do here hurts no one. What I do here is no one's business but mine. I don't pretend to be someone I'm not. Try not to judge people you don't know."

"I'm sorry, Les," Lindsay apologised. "Come on, Anna. You need to leave."

Les shut the door and turned to face him. After approaching Les, Randy hugged him. Strong arms wrapped around him and held him close.

"Anna's just a small town girl, Les. She doesn't know any better." He wasn't sure why he was making excuses for her.

Les snorted. "Small towns aren't the only place you find people like her. They're all over the place, even in big cities, but not here. Not on my ranch or in my home." Les stepped back and met his eyes with a serious gaze. "I can deal with not being able to touch you when we're out in public. I accept not everyone is comfortable with our relationship. My house is different."

Randy took Les' hand and led him to the couch. Sitting down, he encouraged Les to settle next to him. "Thank you," he said, understanding what Les was saying.

"If you want to kiss me, I want you to feel safe enough here to do it. I want my ranch to be a haven for you, baby. I want it to be a place where you don't feel like you need to hide who you are." Les kissed him quick and hard.

"I know and I do feel safe here, but aren't we moving fast?" He had never had a serious relationship and he didn't want to rush into something that wasn't going to last. He didn't want to end up hurting Les, or getting hurt himself.

Les cradled his face in his hands and rubbed a thumb over his bottom lip. "It's strange. You're so mature in some aspects and still very much innocent in others. Maybe I am moving fast, Randy, but I've learnt the hard way that things aren't certain in life. I want you to know how I feel. I'm already half in love with you and it's not a short fall to be all the way in love." A soft kiss was pressed to the corner of his mouth. "I know you're going to feel pressure now and that's not why I told you this. You take all the time you need to figure out how you feel. You've got a couple more weeks here before you head back out on the circuit. Enjoy yourself and don't worry about me."

"I'll try," he consented.

"Good." Les kissed him again then stood up. "I told Margie to pack us a basket for lunch. She should have it ready by now. Let's grab it and go find your spot."

"Great." He got to his feet and followed Les into the kitchen. He was looking forward to spending some time alone with the man.

* * * *

They reined in the horses beside the small stream. Les looked around and smiled. It was a pretty clearing, surrounded by large oak trees. After dismounting, he pulled halters and lead ropes from his saddlebags. By the time he'd got the horses' tack off, Randy had the picket line up. He hooked Sam and Chip to the line, making sure they couldn't get tangled.

"I'm going to take a swim," Randy announced while Les unpacked the other saddlebags.

"Go ahead. I'll be in after I set the food out." He stretched out the blanket and set the bag with the food down.

He turned in time to see Randy's pale ass disappear under the water. Shaking his head, he laughed. He should have known it would be skinny-dipping. After stripping, he stood, soaking up the warm Wyoming sun. So far they had been lucky with the weather—it hadn't been nearly as hot as it could get. All the tension and anger he'd been feeling seeped away, leaving behind contentment.

A cold drop of water splashed on his chest, allowing him a moment to brace himself before his arms were filled with a wet, shivering man. Randy wrapped cool, damp arms around his neck and pulled his head down for a kiss. Putting one hand on the nape of Randy's neck and one on a lean hip, he dived into the kiss. Tongues stroked in and out, imitating the physical act they both were looking forward to. He allowed the eager cowboy to push him back towards the blanket.

Tearing his mouth away from Randy's, he asked, "So I don't get to take a swim?"

"Maybe after lunch. I want a ride." Randy's rough hand slid between them and cupped his balls.

"Wait," he murmured, stepping far enough away so he could kneel on the blanket. It put him at the best height to suck Randy's cock down. Doing a little sucking and licking, he took the man to the edge of climax before he came off Randy. "Do you want to ride me or do I get to ride you?"

"I want you in me," Randy groaned, pushing Les over before dropping down next to him.

Les smiled and lay back, letting his lover take over. His gaze traced the patterns of the leaves against the sky and he thought how perfect this spot was. A sigh came from him as Randy fondled his balls and took just the tip of his shaft in his mouth. He trailed his fingers through Randy's dark curls while the man's head bobbed up and down, working Les' cock like a pro. He wondered where his cowboy had learnt how to give head like that. With a swirl of the tongue and the light scrape of teeth, Randy short-circuited his brain and he decided he didn't care. Les felt his balls tighten, and his climax built in his chest.

"Please…" was all he could say.

"I'll take care of you. Don't worry." Randy dragged the saddlebags over and dug through them. "Ah-ha." He held up the lube and some condoms for Les to see.

Les stroked his own cock while Randy opened the condom wrapper. His hips lifted off the blanket as his lover sheathed his cock with the latex. Randy slicked his own fingers and Les thought he'd come from watching him prepare his ass for Les.

Les grasped Randy's hips as he straddled Les' body. Their groans blended as Randy slowly impaled himself on Les' cock. Les froze and waited until Randy made the first move before he thought about thrusting. Randy rose up with a gentle tightening of his muscles, massaging Les before allowing his ass to drop back down. Les surged up and their bodies slapped together.

Les knew it would only be a few more thrusts like that until he'd be coming. Prising one hand off the lean hips above him, he fisted Randy's curved cock and pumped it in time with their movements.

"Good," Randy grunted.

"I want you to come on my cock, baby," Les ground out as he dragged his palm over the head of Randy's shaft and pressed on the sensitive spot under the crown.

Randy's eyes rolled back in his head and he cried out, cream spilling out over Les' hand. Randy's passage clamped down on Les' shaft and milked his climax from him. Pinning Randy's ass to his groin, he shouted out his release.

When he could think again, Les eased Randy down to his chest and slid out of him. Rolling a little, he managed to bring one side of the blanket up over them and he smoothed the trembling muscles in Randy's back.

"Take a little nap, baby. Lunch can wait for a bit." Les brushed a kiss over the damp curls resting under his chin.

"Sounds good." Randy's lips moved against his chest and Les smiled.

Settling down for a nap of his own, Les found his heart was hoping that the next two weeks went by at a snail's pace.

Chapter Sixteen

Two weeks later

Randy watched Skipper and Buster being loaded into the cattle trailer. The Kaycee rodeo was two days away and the bulls needed to get to the rodeo grounds a day ahead of time to get used to the noises. He'd gone to the doctor's at the beginning of the week and got a clean bill of health. The minute the doctor had told him he could ride, he'd started to feel nervous. Randy knew Les wanted their relationship to continue beyond the last month, but he wasn't sure if the man understood what it was like to love a rodeo man.

Randy knew he'd do whatever he had to do to keep their relationship strong. In the beginning, the fact that Les was his first serious partner had scared him. He'd been afraid he wouldn't be brave enough to stay honest and not hide again.

Arms wrapped around his waist and pulled him tight against a wide chest. Thin lips nibbled on his earlobe.

"What's got you thinking so hard this morning?" Les murmured in his ear.

Sighing, he closed his eyes and soaked in the warmth his lover's body was giving off. It wasn't only warmth he was feeling. It was a flood of security. His heart seemed to believe the world was a safer place when he was sheltered in Les' arms.

"Just a little nervous, I guess." He shrugged. He felt foolish worrying when Les seemed so sure about everything.

"Nervous about what, baby?" Les turned him around and stared down with concerned brown eyes. "You're not worried about riding again, are you?"

He shook his head and looked away. "No, I've been riding all my life. Horses don't scare me."

Les brought his gaze back to him. "Is something scaring you? That's more than just being nervous." Les looked over as Burt walked up to them.

Randy kept his eyes down. He didn't want to upset anyone. It was bad enough Les could tell he was freaking out.

"The bulls are ready to go, boss," Burt informed them.

"Thanks. Why don't you and Dusty head out? I'll ride with Randy and we'll catch up with you." Les squeezed his shoulder as if he was worried Randy would protest.

"Sure, boss. If you don't catch up with us, we'll see you at the hotel." Burt winked at Randy and left.

"Let's go say goodbye to Margie. We'll pick up this conversation when we're on the road." Les kissed him.

"Fine with me," he agreed, and Randy let Les lead him to the main house.

"Margie, we're heading out. Burt, Dusty and I will be home with the bulls Monday night." Les tugged his housekeeper into his arms.

"Lindsay and I will be fine, Master Leslie. Jackson is here as well." She turned to look at Randy. She surprised him by hugging him. "Have a good rodeo, Master Randy. I'll be looking forward to seeing you again soon."

He embraced her while staring at Les over her shoulder. "It might be a while, but I'm planning on returning. I'll be missing your cooking after a few days of fast food." An odd tightness made it hard to swallow. Stepping away, he smiled at her. "Thanks for being so welcoming."

"You're a good man. Don't let anyone tell you different." Her face held a look he remembered seeing on his mother's face when he was little.

"We'd better get going." Les kissed the woman's cheek and took the keys out of his hand. "I'll drive the first half and you'll get the second half, since you know where we need to go."

He stayed quiet as they climbed into his truck. Les waited until they were a few minutes down the road before he started the conversation again.

"So what's got you scared, baby?" Les reached out and put a hand on Randy's knee.

"It's going to be different now." He stared down at Les' hand and thought about how far he'd come in the past month. If a guy had touched him that way before meeting Les, he would have freaked.

"What's going to be different? Us or the rodeo?" A gentle squeeze to his thigh told him that Les wasn't upset.

"The rodeo won't be that hard since you won't be around. I can pretty much act the way I always have."

He covered Les' hand with his and entwined their fingers. "We're going to be different."

"I'm sure we will be."

He liked the way Les didn't deny things were going to change now that he was healthy. "I mean, we've spent most of our time together over the past month. Practically living in each other's back pocket. Now it could be a couple weeks before we see each other again. I've seen rodeo tear relationships apart and I don't want that to happen to us." Swallowing hard, he turned to look out of the window.

Pulling over to the side of the road, Les put the truck in park. Randy was surprised when Les reached over and encouraged him to move closer.

"Why did you stop?" Randy asked.

Les kissed him slow and gentle. Randy moaned when Les' tongue swept into his mouth and stroked his own tongue. After a few minutes of kissing and feeling Les' hands caressing him, Randy relaxed. Les moved a few inches away and smiled down at him.

"We have a few advantages most rodeo couples don't have, baby." Les pressed his thumb to Randy's lips.

"What?" Randy nipped the tip of Les' thumb.

"I have competent men working for me at the ranch. I don't need to be there every hour of every day. That's why I hired Jackson in the first place. I didn't want to do that anymore. I did it for several years after the stables in Virginia became prosperous. I have money. When I want to see you, I can fly to wherever you happen to be on any given weekend." Les winked. "I think I'll be racking up some frequent flyer miles soon."

"You'd do that for me?" He was incredulous. He couldn't remember a time when he had been so important to someone that they would travel to see him, instead of making him come to them.

"Sure, I would. I know what it's like competing in a sport where you're travelling so much in between competitions. I know how some relationships aren't strong enough to survive that kind of separation because the people weren't willing to work at it." Les' face held a serious expression. "I'm committed to this relationship until you tell me you want to move on. I'm willing to take it as fast or as slow as you want it, Randy. There is something you can tell me, though."

"What's that?" He was feeling a little overwhelmed by everything.

"I assume, while we're at the rodeo, I can't touch you. No hugging. No kissing. Nothing that would end up with us getting our asses beat. When you introduce me to people, who do you want me to be? A friend of the family, or what? I've been out for a long time and I can't deny who I am."

Randy started to speak, but Les put a finger on his lips to stop him.

"I'm not about to tell you how to live your life. I know that being out isn't freedom for some people and I'd never out you on purpose. That's why I wanted to know."

He shrugged. "I don't know. I've never had to worry about this sort of thing. Since I've been riding, there's never been a man I've wanted to introduce as anything more than a casual friend. See, that's why I said everything was going to change."

"Don't worry, baby. For now, you tell everyone I'm a friend. They don't need to know anything more than that." Les kissed him once more then let him scoot back into his seat. "We better get going. Burt and Dusty have a good lead on us."

"Thank you," he said softly.

Les winked at him and laughed. "As long as you realise I'm not going anywhere, I've got all the time in the world."

Randy laughed as well and settled into his seat. He turned on the radio and the soft twang of Chris LeDoux came out of the speakers. His nerves and worries were gone. At that moment, life couldn't get any better. He was on his way to ride broncs in a rodeo, listening to good music with the man he could easily fall in love with at his side.

* * * *

"Hey, Les, wake up. We're here."

Les opened his eyes to see Randy leaning over him and shaking his shoulder. Sitting up, he climbed stiffly out of the truck and stretched. His joints popped and he grimaced as his stiff muscles protested riding in the truck for several hours. He glanced around the hotel parking lot and didn't see the ranch truck.

"Where's Dusty and Burt?" he inquired.

Randy smiled. "I called them when we hit town. They're still out at the rodeo grounds, settling the bulls in. They ran into some friends, so they won't be meeting us for dinner, though they did invite us to join them later on at Buddy's. It's a local bar."

"Sounds good to me, if you want to go. Right now I want to check in and take a shower. I need some hot water to soak my tired old body in."

"You look good wet." Randy leered at him.

Blushing, he punched the cowboy in the arm. "Flattery will get you kissed."

"I was hoping it might get me laid," Randy admitted with a chuckle.

"I'm sure that can be arranged." He wanted to kiss those smiling lips so badly, but he knew better than to do it out in the parking lot. "Let's get our room."

Ten minutes later, they were setting their bags down inside. Two queen-sized beds dominated the space. Les sat down on one.

"Shit," he groaned as he leaned over to take his boots off.

"Here, let me." Randy knelt at his feet and grabbed the heel of Les' boot to tug it off.

"Thanks, baby." He ruffled the hat-flattened curls on Randy's head. "Screwed up my back a while ago. Now, if I sit for a long time, it stiffens up on me."

"Did it happen when you had your head injury?" Randy pulled the other boot off and then stood, offering Les a hand.

Shaking his head, he took the calloused hand and let Randy lift him from the bed. "No, it was an earlier fall I took when I was fourteen. Fractured a vertebra and was in a brace for seven months. It healed enough for me to ride again. Just likes to remind me that I'm not getting any younger."

Randy unbuttoned Les' shirt. "Let's get you out of your clothes and in the shower. The hot water should loosen you up a little."

He was happy to let Randy take care of him—it had been several years since a handsome man had wanted to help him with anything. He rested against the counter in the bathroom while Randy turned on the water. Soon steam was fogging up the mirror and he could feel the heat filling the area.

"Go ahead. Climb in. I'm going to order some food. That'll give us some time to rest before we head over to Buddy's." Randy headed towards the phone.

"So you want to go to the bar?" Les shouted over the pounding shower.

"I know the guys Burt and Dusty ran into. It's sort of a routine we have. Most of us get into town a day or two before the rodeo starts and we meet up at one of the local bars. Play some pool, dance and drink. It's a way to relax before the fun really starts." Randy's voice got closer.

Les smiled as the shower curtain slid open and Randy joined him under the water. A moan filled the air when strong hands connected with his back. Bracing himself against the shower wall, he dropped his head to rest on the tiles.

Randy's warm breath brushed over his ear. "We'll get those muscles feeling better. I'm going to want to do some dancing with you tonight."

"This isn't a gay bar we're going to, is it?" he asked.

"No, but we can do a little dancing when we get back." Randy's hands caressed his hips once before going back to massaging him. "I bet you're a great dancer."

"Used to be. Haven't done it for a while." He thought back to the last time he'd been dancing. In Ocala, Florida, the night before the Grand Prix, he and Taylor had gone out to have some fun. They'd danced and made love that night. It had been the last time for a lot of things. The next day he'd been injured and his life had never been the same again.

A nip at the nape of his neck reminded him he had a new lover who wouldn't leave him because he was scarred. "Maybe we'll take off after your season is done and head to San Francisco. We'll dance in some of the clubs there."

"Sounds good to me." Randy soaped up his hands and washed Les down.

By the time they were done with their shower, Les was hard. He knew he could tempt Randy into bed for a quickie, but he decided to let the lust build before they took care of it. Stepping out of the bathroom, he heard room service knock on the door.

"Supper's here," he said as Randy came into the room.

"Good. I'm starved." Randy joined him at the small table.

He watched Randy inhale the steak and fries. Making his way through half his own steak, he handed the rest to Randy when the other man's plate was clean. "Here, you can have the rest of mine."

"Are you sure?" Randy reached for the food.

"I'm not that hungry and I'm not drinking tonight, so I don't need a full stomach." He settled back to wait for Randy to finish.

Chapter Seventeen

Randy led the way into Buddy's. The noise hit them like a physical wave, but it wasn't so loud that he'd end up with a headache by the end of the night. A haze of smoke hung over the bar. Stopping just inside the door, he looked around, trying to find Dusty and Burt. He felt the fleeting touch of Les' hand on his ass. Tonight was going to be hard. He wanted to drag Les out on the dance floor and plaster his body against the muscular man.

"Hey, kid, get the hell over here." Dusty waved from the back of the bar where two pool tables were.

He reached out to take Les' hand and stopped just in time. Damn. He was going to have to get used to being out in the real world now. Randy gestured with his hand.

"Take the lead. I'll follow," Les told him with an understanding gleam in his eyes.

He nodded, then made his way through the crowd, greeting other cowboys he knew as he went. Finally, they arrived at the table where Burt, Dusty and five other men were sat. Dusty pulled out a chair for him.

Les grabbed a chair from a nearby table and turned it around to straddle it and rest his arms on the back of it. A pretty waitress came to take their order.

"What can I get you, gentlemen?" Her eyes passed over Randy and landed on Les.

Randy saw the flare of interest in her gaze. He hid his smile with his hand. Les grinned up at her.

"I'll take a soda," Les ordered.

"No beer? I thought that was standard drinking fare for a cowboy," she flirted.

"Well, I'm not a cowboy, not really." Les winked at her. "Doctor's orders, I'm afraid." He tapped the dent in his head.

"Oh, wow." She reached out to touch the white streak in Les' dark hair.

Randy felt a growl start in his throat. A nudge from Dusty kept him from knocking her hand away from his partner. Les shot him a glance while he was leaning away from her.

"Sorry. I'm a little touchy about it." He grinned apologetically.

"I understand. How'd it happen?" She hugged her tray to her chest and looked like she was settling in for a nice chat.

"Missy, do you think you could get our drinks or do we need to get kicked in the head for you to wait on us?" Lou joked.

She blushed, but turned to the rest of them. "You could get some manners, Lou."

They gave her their drink orders and watched her stroll off. A couple of the guys whistled. Dusty chuckled then leant forward to look around Randy at Les.

"Hey, boss, the bulls settled in real good. We'll see how well they deal with the noise and stuff as more people arrive tomorrow," Dusty informed him.

Randy relaxed. There was no reason to get upset about Missy flirting with Les. The man was good-looking, which was sure to attract females. He imagined he would have to fight the guys off when they went out to the clubs. Les was saying something to Dusty, but all Randy felt was the warmth of Les' shoulder as his lover leaned against him.

"Cowboys, this is my boss, Les Hardin. Boss, these are the worst bunch of rodeo men you'll ever meet. They can introduce themselves to you." Burt waved to the other five men at the table with them.

"Cy, how are Patty and the kids doing?" Randy had been out of the loop for a month. He needed to catch up on the gossip.

"The kids are doing great. Patty's pregnant again." Cy's cheeks turned red as the guys teased him.

"How many do you have?" Les moved slightly, brushing up against Randy.

The casual touch shot straight to Randy's cock and it filled to press against his zipper as if it were begging to get out. Shifting, he tried to adjust himself and find a more comfortable position. Moving closer, Les reached for his glass and Randy breathed in the earthy scent he'd come to associate with his lover. He had to get away from the man for a few minutes or else he wouldn't be able to walk out of the bar without embarrassing himself. In a panic, he looked around and saw one of the pool tables was free. He jumped to his feet and glanced at the guys.

"Anyone want to play some pool?" His voice was husky. He hoped the others thought it was the smoke causing it.

Les, Burt and Dusty smirked at him. A young bull rider, Tony, stood as well.

"I'll play," Tony said as he walked to the table.

"Good." Randy hurried to get a cue. Standing on the other side of the table from Les, he tried to get control of his desire. He couldn't be sporting a hard-on every time they went places. At some point, someone would comment on it and there was no way he could say he was turned on by the man with him.

"You want to break?" Tony looked up at him from under the brim of his black cowboy hat.

"No, you can." Randy studied his opponent.

Tony Romanos was a new addition to the rodeo circuit. He'd started shortly before Randy was injured. He was a private guy and didn't really join in with the practical jokes and teasing. This was the first time Randy could remember him coming to the bar with the rest of them. Tony was stocky and muscular like all good bull riders were. With dark eyes and hair, he was good-looking and Randy was sure the women flocked around him.

Tony broke the balls and sank a solid. Missing his next shot, he came around to Randy's side of the table and rested a hip on a stool nearby. Randy rubbed chalk on the tip of his cue while studying his shot. Tony took out a cigarette and lit it.

"Can I ask you something without you kicking the shit out of me?" Tony's voice was low and muffled as he held the cigarette between his lips.

Intrigued, Randy glanced over at the cowboy. Serious dark eyes stared back at him. He saw an emotion in them he couldn't name, but it was one that looked familiar.

"Sure. I don't feel like getting into a fight tonight. Got other things planned." He shot a look over at Les.

"I bet. Is he yours?" Tony nodded towards Les.

"Mine?" Unease trickled into his stomach.

"Yours, as in are you fucking him?" Keeping his voice low, Tony took a drag on his cigarette.

"Why are you asking?" Randy turned to face him, blocking out everyone else.

"Being polite, man. I don't want to make a move on your guy." Tony smiled.

"I didn't know you went that way." Randy stalled. He realised his answer to Tony's question would determine the rest of his life in the rodeo.

Shrugging, Tony laughed. "It's not something you bring up in conversation with a bunch of cowboys around, kid. Most of the time, I figure it's between a man and his God. I just want to make sure I'm not encroaching on your territory if I make a play for Hardin."

"How can you be sure he isn't going to beat your ass if you made that move?" Randy wondered.

"After you've been out for a while, you start to develop a feeling for the ones who are like you." Tony's gaze dropped to the floor then back up at Randy. "I knew you were gay the minute I met you and, if you'd been willing to play, I'd have asked you out."

Randy felt like he'd been punched in the stomach. Had he been that obvious?

Tony must have seen the worry in Randy's eyes because the cowboy reached out a hand and waved to make him look at him. "I told you, I know these things. Most of the guys haven't noticed, and probably wouldn't care if they did know. I could tell you were still in the closet and I'm not about to push someone into revealing something they don't want to." Tony threw a look over Randy's shoulder. "If you don't want to tell me, that's cool. I'll leave it alone."

Randy took a deep breath. Moving to stand beside Tony, they looked at Les. His lover caught them staring and raised an eyebrow at him. With a smile, Randy stepped out of the closet for the last time. "Yes, he's mine."

Les blushed then nodded slightly, letting him know he'd read his lips. Tony groaned good-naturedly.

"Damn. I should have moved on you when I had a chance." Tony gave Les and him a once-over. "You're both very lucky guys. Your turn."

"Thanks, Tony." Randy went and lined up his shot.

They played three games, with Tony winning two of them. By the time they got back to the table, Les seemed to have fit in with the others. People who rode the rodeo were a close-knit family—they understood how rough the sport was on everyone involved. They were friendly people and willing to give everything to help someone out, but if you were a wannabe there was a wall between you and the true rodeo.

"I admit to being a rodeo novice. I don't understand it, which is why I grabbed Burt and Dusty when they showed up. I needed help getting the right type of bulls for my rough stock." Les said as he handed Randy another beer, sitting down next to him.

"If you don't know anything about the rodeo, why bucking bulls?" Lou waved Missy down and ordered another round.

"Why not? I've always believed variety was the way to success. Diversify and you won't have put all your eggs in one basket, in case someone drops the basket." Les shrugged. "My ranch raises and trains cutting horses and bucking bulls right now. Who knows what we might decide to do next year?"

"How did you and Les meet?" Tony lit up another cigarette after asking the question.

"When I got out of the hospital a month ago, I decided to head home and see if I could finish healing up there. No such luck. On my way out of town, I ran into Les. His ranch butts up against the Rocking H and he was nice enough to let me crash at his place." Randy told as much of the truth as he thought they wanted to know.

"He got a bed and the wonderful cooking of my housekeeper. I got some expert advice on my cutting horses. It was a fair trade." Les lifted his glass to Randy in a toast.

Randy felt his face warm and he hoped the bar was too dark for the men to see he was blushing. He'd got a bed all right. It was a king-sized bed filled with the hottest man he'd ever seen. He looked down the table at Tony. The bull rider winked at him and grinned.

* * * *

The group broke up around midnight and they headed back to the hotel. Dusty and Burt drove back to the rodeo grounds to check on the bulls once more before going to bed. Randy couldn't wait to get to their room. His hard-on had got worse throughout the night—getting to sit so close to Les but not touching him had turned him on so much his cock ached.

"I like your friends," Les said as he opened the hotel door.

Pushing him in, Randy whipped him around and slammed him back against the door. Les didn't have time to say anything as Randy's mouth crashed into his. Les felt his lip split under the fierceness of

Randy's kiss. Tangling his hands in the dark curls, he tugged Randy away from him.

"What the hell's gotten into you?" He frowned.

Randy's eyes focused on the drop of blood welling from Les' lip. "I'm sorry. Not being able to touch you all night drove me crazy." Trembling fingers touched him gently.

"Nothing to apologise for, baby. Just warn me next time before you jump me." Les eased Randy's mouth back down to his.

This time his mouth was taken with slow determination. Shivers raced down his spine as Randy's tongue teased the roof of his mouth. Randy sucked on his tongue while working to unbutton his shirt. He ran his hands down the lean back to cup Randy's ass, lifting it up so their erections would fit together.

Randy wrapped one of his long legs around his and rocked his hips forward, rubbing against him. Les could tell by the way Randy was moaning and moving that the cowboy would be coming soon.

"Just a second, baby." He managed to move them apart a few inches so he could fit his hand in between them.

Unbuttoning and unzipping turned into a dexterity test because Randy couldn't seem to stay still. Each innocent brush of his hand over Randy's groin made Randy groan and jerk.

His groans joined in when he fisted their cocks together and started pumping. At first the friction of his dry palm stroking their heated flesh caused pleasurable pain. After a few tugs, the pre-cum leaking from their slits slicked his hand enough to make it move easily and quickly. Les felt his balls tighten and he spread his legs to give them better support.

Randy threw back his head and cried out, "Les."

"That's it, baby. Come for me. I want to feel your cum all over my stomach," Les ordered.

Hot heat flooded over his hand and skin. He watched Randy's face contort into a grimace of lustful pain. Then his climax shot through him. He set his head back on the door and grunted as his own cum mixed with Randy's on his skin. He continued pumping until he was sure they were both done. Randy unwound his leg from his and Les lowered him so he could touch the floor. He gathered his lover close and nuzzled his mouth into the sweat-soaked curls.

"Are you feeling a little better?" he whispered.

"Mmm. Much better. Except now I want to take a shower. We're all sticky." Randy pushed away from him and started undressing.

Les followed his example. "A shower sounds good. Afterwards we can find out which bed is better for having a little fun on."

Randy's eager grin made him laugh as he headed into the bathroom. He knew it wouldn't take long for Randy to recover for another round.

Chapter Eighteen

On Sunday afternoon, Les found himself sitting in the stands for the final round of the bareback competition. Randy had the overall lead going into the short go and had managed to win the go-around the night before with the highest score. Les was happy to see that the injuries didn't seem to be bothering Randy.

He smiled at the older couple sitting down next to him. He'd found the people who came to watch the rodeos were rather friendly, even to perfect strangers. Relaxing against the bleacher behind him, he pushed down his hat to rest for a few minutes before the bucking started. He and Randy had been up rather late the night before, celebrating Randy's winnings.

"Tee, look. Randy Hersch is riding. I wish we'd known he would be here. I'd have had David come with us." Les overheard the lady say to her husband.

"I don't know if that would have even made him come, Beth. He doesn't like coming to these things now that he's not riding anymore." The man's voice held sadness and a little annoyance.

"Maybe we should go and say hi to Randy after the round," Beth suggested.

Les sat up and pushed his hat back. Turning to the couple, he smiled. "My name's Les Hardin. I'm a friend of Randy's. How do you know him?"

"I'm Timothy Preston, but everyone calls me Tee. This is my wife, Beth. Our son David used to be Randy's travelling partner while David was competing." Tee shook Les' hand while introducing himself and his wife.

"Really? Randy never said anything about having someone travel with him." Les didn't know if he was feeling jealous or just surprised.

"David got injured at the beginning of the season. I guess you could say he retired from the rodeo." Beth's blue eyes held the same sadness as her husband's voice. "David and Randy started on the circuit at the same time, so it just made sense for them to travel together. Gave them someone to hang out with and talk to. It helped to split costs between them as well."

"May I ask how David was injured?" Les wasn't sure he really wanted to know, since it would just add to his worry about Randy.

"He came off a horse and landed on his neck. Broke his back. He can walk and all, but the shock of riding a bronc could cause enough damage he'd be paralysed if he tried. So he retired and hasn't been the same since." Beth sighed. Tee reached out and took his wife's hand.

"All he ever wanted to do was ride broncs. We took him to his first rodeo when he was seven and all he talked about from that moment on was winning the World Championship in bareback riding. Being told he couldn't do what he loved anymore sort of broke something inside him." Tee gave an embarrassed laugh. "I'm sorry. We've dumped all our troubles on you."

"It's all right," Les assured them. He took his hat off and pointed to his scar. "I understand what it's like to have your dreams taken away from you. I used to ride jumpers. About six years ago at a show, my horse slipped landing a jump. I came off and he nailed me in the head. Without my helmet and the agility of that same horse, I'd be dead. As it is, I can't compete anymore." He usually didn't talk about it to total strangers, but something about this couple told him they would understand and he sympathised with their absent son.

"Oh, my." Beth reached out and touched the skin right before it started its concave dive into his skull. "That couldn't have been a pleasant experience."

He chuckled. "No. I was in a coma for six months and then I had to learn how to eat, walk and talk again. When I was finally healthy enough, I headed out west to try my hand at something else. My ranch runs alongside Randy's. That's how we met."

"Is he doing all right?" Beth asked.

"He's coming back after being off for a while owing to an injury, but it seems like it hasn't slowed him down any. He's in first coming into the short go." He looked over at the chutes. "It looks like they're getting ready to start."

They cheered and shouted as each competitor rode. Les found Tee a fount of information on what made a good bucking horse. A plan started to form, but he wanted to talk to Randy before he put it in action. During a break in the competition, he asked Tee, "Can he ride?"

"Sure, he can. Just not bucking horses. Too much bouncing and stuff like that." Tee sighed. "At times all he does is ride. He's gone in the morning when we get up and doesn't come back until after dark. I wish there was something I could do to get him interested again."

"The hardest part of living is getting interested in something else when you've lost the most important thing to you." He understood how David felt.

The bareback riding started up again. Soon it was down to Randy, who was riding last since he was in first place. Les tensed. He hated watching the horse burst from the gate, kicking and hopping its way across the arena. He winced with each violent jerk on Randy's hand. He felt pain in his neck with each quick snap of Randy's head.

Eight seconds later and the pick-up man helped Randy off the horse. Yelling, Les stood up and waved his hat in the air. He had told Randy where he'd be sitting and his lover looked over at him. Giving him a thumbs-up, Randy smiled and headed back behind the chutes.

"Eighty-seven point five, ladies and gentlemen. Randy Hersch has done it again. He's won the day money and the all-around money. Good job, Hersch. It's nice to see you back. Let's show the young man our appreciation." The announcer congratulated Randy.

Beth and Tee cheered along with Les. Turning to the couple, he asked, "Would you like to join Randy and me for dinner tonight?"

"We'd love to see Randy again. Thank you," Beth accepted for them.

He made plans to meet them at a local restaurant. He figured Randy would know where it was. After saying goodbye, he tilted his hat down and climbed off the bleachers. He nodded and waved to people he had met during the weekend. They seemed to have accepted him as Randy's family.

He stopped just outside the area where the cowboys prepared for their rides. Leaning against the fence, he watched Randy accept the congratulations from the other men.

"Hey, Les, come to collect your guy?" Tony grinned as the bull rider joined him at the fence.

"I thought I'd let him enjoy his success for a while before I pull him away." Les caught Randy's eye and nodded.

"It's good to see him back. I'm surprised he came back, though, now that he has you." Tony tapped a cigarette out of the pack and lit it.

"What do you mean?" Puzzled, he frowned at the man.

"We both know Randy isn't a die-hard rodeo man. He's not going to stick around riding broncs until he's too old. I've heard of your ranch. You're getting a reputation for training good cutting horses. A few more years and you'll be the man to see about getting champion cutters. If there's one thing Randy loves, it's horses." Tony shot Les a glance from under his hat brim. "And maybe you."

Les didn't deny or confirm what Tony had said. "Randy knows there's always a place at my ranch for him, but he isn't ready to stop following the rodeo. I'm not about to push him either."

"He isn't ready to trust that you won't hurt him or turn away from him." Tony turned to stare at the young bronc rider. "I've been on my own a lot longer than Randy has. I left home when I was fifteen. Just couldn't take it anymore. By the time I was sixteen, I knew I was gay and didn't try denying or hiding it. Didn't see the point. I got my ass kicked a few times, but mostly I was left alone. I learnt the hard way that people will hurt you. It's easier for them to hurt you than to care for you."

Les didn't know what to say. He could say he didn't plan on hurting Randy and it would be true, but he'd never be able to promise that he'd never do it in the future. Sometimes people got hurt no matter what the good intentions were.

"I don't think you'll hurt him. You'd probably hurt yourself before you broke his heart. As cynical as I am, I know there are guys out there like you, Les, and Randy's a lucky man to have found you." Tony slapped him on the shoulder and nodded to Randy as the bull rider moved away.

"Great ride, man." Les stared down into the sparkling blue eyes of his lover and clamped down on the urge to kiss those smiling lips.

"Thanks. Are you interested in celebrating with me?" A sly grin crossed Randy's face.

"I might be convinced to help you savour your triumphant return." He gestured for Randy to lead the way to the truck.

Randy was so excited, he practically bounced on the balls of his feet. Les followed the tight cowboy butt swaying in front of him. He bit his tongue to keep from whistling.

To keep his mind away from the image of Randy's ass filling his hands, he said, "I met the Prestons today. I asked them to meet us for dinner tonight."

"Really? Was David with them?" Randy climbed into the truck while he asked.

"No. From what they said, he doesn't come to rodeos anymore. He mostly just rides his horse and is antisocial." Les started the truck and pulled out of the parking lot.

Randy was quiet for a moment. "That's not surprising. When you had your back injury, how would you have reacted to being told you could never compete again?"

"I wouldn't have wanted to live. I'd have isolated myself so I could brood and be mad at the world." He smiled and winked at Randy. "If I hadn't been so concerned with trying to survive when I got out of the coma, I would have done all those things."

"I don't blame either of you. For David, bronc riding was all he ever wanted to do. His dad used to raise bucking horses. He grew up around the rodeo. Now, watching one from the stands reminds him of everything he lost." Randy reached out and rested his hand on Les' thigh.

"I was impressed with how much knowledge Tee Preston had about the horses. You said he used to raise bucking stock?" He knew it and the information Randy was giving him would help him make up his mind.

"Yeah. Their stock company went bust. Bad business deals with crooked dealers and things like that. His dad works for a neighbouring rancher now." His lover shook his head. "Sad situation."

"I never told you about my plans to expand the rough stock part of the ranch, did I?" He kept his gaze on the road, but, out of the corner of his eye, he noticed the narrowed glance Randy threw at him.

"What are you talking about?"

"The bulls were just the first part of the plan. I wanted to see how they did. I think we're on the right track with them."

Randy squeezed his leg. "Get to the point, Les."

"I thought David and his dad would be perfect to help me start my bucking horse programme."

Randy stayed silent until they pulled up outside the hotel. Les parked the truck and turned it off. He faced Randy and found that he was already staring back at him.

"What?" He squirmed.

"You just can't help it, can you?" Randy gave him a shy smile.

"Can't help what?"

"Picking up strays and undesirables." Randy hopped down from the truck.

Les scrambled after him. "Every creature I've picked up has been useful in some way. I don't believe that just because you're broken, you're useless." He stood beside Randy, waiting while his lover opened their room door.

"You do know why you do this, don't you?" Randy pushed the door open and went in.

Les sat on one of the beds. Flopping back, he looked up at the bland white ceiling. "Of course I do. I knew the deep meaning behind this long before my therapist analysed me. I'm doing it to prove Taylor wrong. I need to know that what he said about me wasn't true. I take a person or creature in and hope they'll grow. I watch them get better. I want them to thrive despite obstacles others might consider challenges."

Randy claimed the other bed. Leaning forward, he rested his elbows on his knees. "Is that why you took me in?"

"Partly, yes." There was no point in lying. "It's a deep part of who I am now, baby. A part I can't shut off. I don't want to shut it off. When I take someone in, I give them attention and care. They all leave when they're better and normally that doesn't bother me." He reached across the space and took Randy's hands in his. "I don't want you to leave. In the short time you've been with me, you've wormed your way into my heart."

"You want to save David and his father." It was a statement, not a question.

"Yes, I do. Don't think I made up the bucking horse idea on a whim. I've been thinking about it for a while. Ask Dusty or Burt."

"If you can do it without hurting their pride, I say go for it."

Les decided he was done talking. Kneeling in front of Randy, he helped him take off his boots. Randy leant back and braced his upper body on his elbows. Les slid his hands up jean-clad thighs, spreading them wider to accommodate his shoulders. He worked his thumbs along the sides of the bulge in the front of Randy's pants. Leaning down, he placed an open-mouthed kiss on the fabric and blew warm air over it.

Randy's head fell back and his throat swallowed convulsively. Moving his mouth over the erection, Les unbuckled Randy's belt and unbuttoned his jeans. He rose a little higher on his knees and took the zipper pull in his teeth. With gentle tugs, making sure nothing got caught, he unzipped the fabric. The wet, swollen head of Randy's cock pushed against Les' chin.

"Lift your hips," he ordered as he pushed his hands into the waistband of the jeans.

Not saying anything, Randy arched his hips off the bed, allowing Les to strip the tight denim off. He tossed them over his shoulder while sucking the tip of Randy's cock into his mouth.

"Oh," Randy gasped.

Les swirled his tongue around the crown of the shaft and played with the slit. He swallowed the bitter, salty pre-cum filling his mouth. Relaxing his muscles, he sucked the curved cock all the way down to the base. Randy fell back on the bed and grunted. Les loved the fact he could blow the cowboy's mind until there was nothing left but noises.

He pressed his tongue against the vein on the underside of Randy's dick. He started moving slow and easy, up and down, while sucking hard. Soon, the lean hips beneath his hands were writhing in time with him.

"Les, gonna come. Gonna come soon." Randy's voice was harsh with desire.

Les grabbed his hand and wrapped it around the base of Randy's cock. "Hold tight. I don't want you to come until I'm in you." He quickly tore off his clothes and found a condom—he opened it and rolled it over his own aching cock. Wasting no time, he slicked his shaft and stretched Randy so there wouldn't be any pain.

"That feels so good," Randy whimpered, his hips rolling, fucking himself on Les' fingers.

Pulling out, Les replaced his fingers with his cock. He shoved in hard and deep, making Randy cry out.

"Shit."

While he reamed Randy's ass and made sure to nail the cowboy's gland with every thrust, he tugged Randy's cock. Scraping a thumbnail lightly over the sensitive head had Randy bucking and moaning.

Les leaned in and whispered, "I want to feel you come, baby."

"Les," Randy shouted.

Strings of cum coated his hand and the rippling stomach beneath him. Randy's tight ass clamped down and milked his own release. Grunting, he rode through Randy's climax and filled the condom as the aftershocks were dying out. He collapsed on the sweat-drenched body below him. Kissing Randy gently, he thanked him.

"I'll grab a towel. We'll clean up and take a nap. We have enough time to catch Tony in the bull riding event before we meet the Prestons for dinner."

They both groaned as Les pulled out. He padded to the bathroom and cleaned up before he brought back a warm damp towel and washed Randy, afterwards he tossed the towel in the general direction of the bathroom. He helped Randy move to the other bed where he cuddled close to his lover under the blankets. Randy was already asleep by the time Les had set the alarm.

He kissed the stubble-roughened cheek close to him and whispered, "Congratulations, love."

Chapter Nineteen

Randy cheered as Tony started spurring the bull he was riding. The buzzer sounded and the man bailed. Racing to the fence, Tony got to the top before the bull could hook him.

"Great job, Romanos," Randy called.

Somehow Tony heard him over the shouting of the crowd. Catching his eye, the young bull rider nodded and smiled. Those dark eyes looked over at Les and winked.

"He's a flirt, isn't he?" Les laughed.

"Yes." Randy wondered why Tony's continuous flirting wasn't upsetting him.

"Are you mad because he flirts with me?" Les asked in a low voice as they made their way down the bleachers.

"No. I trust you and, as surprising as it might seem, I trust Tony as well. He might be attracted to you but, as long as we're together, he'll never make a move." He turned to head back behind the chutes. "Let's go congratulate the lucky bastard."

A crowd of cowboys surrounded Tony when they got there. The moment the bull rider saw them, he excused himself and came over to them.

"Congratulations, man. A win here puts you in fifth position in the standings, doesn't it?" Randy shook Tony's hand.

"Hell, yeah. A few more wins and I'll be in first heading into the finals." Tony gripped his hand tight.

Randy got the feeling, if people weren't surrounding them, Tony would have hugged them both.

"Randy and I are having dinner with some friends of his. Would you like to join us?" Les stood close to Randy, so Randy could feel the back of the man's hand brush his hip.

"Thanks, but I'm meeting some of the guys over at Buddy's. Gonna do some celebrating. Maybe I'll catch you tomorrow." Tony winked at them again and walked off.

Randy chuckled as he and Les headed to their truck. "He's a trip."

"Tony's a good guy," Les agreed.

Randy unlocked the truck and climbed behind the wheel. Watching Les slide in on the other side, he sighed. Les' dark brown eyes met his with a question in them.

"Just thinking that I'm going to miss having you around all the time." A twinge of sadness rushed through him.

Les touched his hand resting on the seat between them. "You can call me every night and I'm pretty sure I can make it to some of the rodeos on the weekends. That's the beauty of dating a rich man. I don't have to worry about making money." Les squeezed his hand. "It's not like I'm going overseas or something like that, baby. It'll be okay."

Randy started the truck and pulled out of the parking lot. Tangling his fingers with Les' again, he held tight as he drove to the restaurant where they were meeting David's parents. "I hope David will be there. I haven't talked to him in six months. Since he retired, he cut himself off from his rodeo friends."

"I asked them to bring him along. I knew you would like to talk to him and I want him there when I propose my rough stock idea." Grimacing, Les pushed his black cowboy hat back and touched the scar on his head.

"Have a headache?" Randy stopped at a stop sign and glanced over at his lover.

"Just a slight one. I'll take a pill at the restaurant. It should be fine." Les rested his head back on the seat.

Randy knew better than to make a big deal of it. Les had been coping with the headaches for longer than Randy had known him, so if he wasn't concerned about the pain, he wouldn't be either.

A few minutes later, they pulled into the restaurant parking lot. Excitement shot through Randy when he saw David standing outside the building smoking a cigarette.

"He's here," he exclaimed as he piled out of the truck.

Les climbed out a little slower, seeming to hold his head and back stiff. Randy raced up to David.

"David, it's great to see you." He caught the man in a bear hug.

David hugged him back with less enthusiasm. "Well, when Mom and Dad told me your friend invited them to dinner with y'all, I had to come. Just to see how you were doing."

"I'm doing great." He turned to see Les joining them. "Les, this is my old travelling companion. David, this is a good friend of mine, Les Hardin."

"It's good to meet you, Mr Hardin." David held out his hand.

"It's nice meeting you as well," Les ground out between clenched teeth.

Randy shot his lover a worried glance. David had a puzzled look on his face.

"Are your parents here?" Randy covered Les' lukewarm greeting.

"They're inside. We got a table in non-smoking, so I came out to have one last cigarette before dinner." David held up the half-finished smoke.

"I'm going to go in and get something to drink. I promise I'll be much better company after I take my medicine." Les inclined his head slightly and went inside.

"A little stiff, isn't he?" David sounded unimpressed with Les.

"It's an old injury. He gets terrible headaches. I think the sun and excitement today were a bit much for him. He'll be fine once he takes his pills." Randy was concerned, but he didn't think Les would want him hovering around him. "So what have you been doing since you retired?"

"Nothing, except riding around the ranch. I can't seem to concentrate enough to figure out what I want to do. Rodeo was all I ever wanted. Now that that's gone, I'm lost." He glared out into the street.

Randy wished he understood what he was going through, but he wasn't in love with the rodeo. It was a job, pure and simple. Something that gave him enough money to survive and a way to never have to see his father. "You never know. An opportunity might get thrown into your lap soon. Let's head in."

David threw his cigarette to the ground and crushed it with his heel. Going inside, they found Les sitting with Tee and Beth. Randy sat next to Les and settled a gentle hand on the man's thigh.

"You okay?" he asked in a low voice.

"I took some pills. Just have to wait until they kick in." Les looked at the Prestons. "Forgive me if I'm not a hundred per cent at the moment. There are side effects from my injury and I'm dealing with one of them now."

"We understand." Tee spoke for his family.

Beth looked at Randy and smiled. "Randy, how have you been?"

"Good, Mrs Preston." He grinned at her while keeping a concerned eye on Les. "I'm starting to ride again after a wreck a month or so ago."

They talked about people they knew and he got David to join in on the gossip. It wasn't until their dinner arrived that the tension left Les' shoulders and a smile graced the man's face.

"Mr Preston, Randy tells me you used to own bucking horses." Les joined their chatting.

Tee looked surprised by the change in the subject but he nodded. "Yes. It was a good business. We had a few bad breaks."

"Would you and David be interested in forming a business partnership with me to breed and raise bucking horses?"

"You're fucking joking," David burst out.

"David, watch your mouth," Beth admonished.

"No, I'm not joking. It'll be the same sort of deal I worked out with Burt Tackett and Dusty Spiess." Les sipped his coffee.

Randy didn't say anything. He didn't know what kind of agreement Les had with the ex-bull riders, but, knowing his lover, it had to be fair and profitable for all involved.

David shot Randy a glance. "Is he for real?"

"Just listen to what Les has to say," he suggested.

"Keep talking, Mr Hardin." Tee sat forward in his chair, interest gleaming in his eyes.

"To start with, I'll own sixty per cent of the company because I'll be supplying the capital. You'll be getting twenty per cent each for what you know about bucking horses. As the programme becomes more successful, you'll gain a bigger percentage until you'll own forty-five per cent each and I'll retain ten," Les explained.

Randy thought it was a reasonable deal. He let his gaze linger on Les' face for a moment. He was relieved to see the pain lines had faded. He squeezed Les' thigh and the muscle under his hand flexed.

"You don't want any money from us?" David was sceptical, Randy could tell by the tilt of his friend's head.

"I don't need your money. I have more than enough to buy thirty top-end horses and have them turn out to be duds. If I sold them for a loss, it wouldn't make a dent in my income. I have the money. What I don't have is the expertise to pick the good ones." Les' expression was serious as he looked both David then his father in the eyes. "I like making money. I'm not interested in get-rich-quick schemes. I want solid businesses that will continue to grow and make more money every year."

Father and son stared at each other for a moment. David shrugged, leaving the decision to his father.

"Well, Mr Hardin, I'll need to think on it," Tee hedged.

Seeing Les grin, Randy realised his lover knew the Prestons would say yes. Les gave him a look and Randy had the feeling he might not like what the man was going to say next.

"There are two things I have to tell you that might influence your decision. First of all, my foreman is African-American. You'll be dealing with him a lot."

"Doesn't matter as long as he's a good guy," David commented.

"Tammy's dating him," Randy interjected.

"Your sister always seemed level-headed." David stabbed a piece of his steak.

"Second of all, I'm gay. If that makes you uncomfortable, I won't be having my lawyer draw up a contract."

Tee and Beth looked surprised, but Randy saw David eyeing him thoughtfully. After a moment of silence, Tee laughed.

"I can think of a dozen other reasons to not like someone. David?" Tee asked his son.

A sly smile crossed David's face. "I don't know, Dad. Do you have a boyfriend, Hardin?"

Randy could feel his face flushing and was glad that the restaurant's lighting was low, though he knew David's eagle eye had caught his blush.

"David Preston," Beth gasped in horrified embarrassment. "I'm sorry, Mr Hardin, I thought I raised him better than that."

"Please call me Les and it's all right, ma'am." Les drew David's gaze away from Randy. "I have someone very important in my life at the moment, but you don't need to know who he is."

David ducked his head. "Sorry, Hardin. I was teasing."

"I know, but for some people it isn't a laughing matter." Les signalled to the waiter. "Order fresh drinks and we'll toast to what I hope will soon be an exciting new business venture for all of us."

* * * *

Randy went to get the truck while Les paid the bill. David followed him. Lighting a cigarette, his friend blew out a puff of smoke.

David wasn't looking at Randy when he asked, "Are you Hardin's someone special?"

Randy felt the same way he had with Tony. This moment was another small step away from the dark place he'd always hidden in. Staring up at the bright stars, he admitted, "Yes, I am."

Out of the corner of his eye, he saw David nod.

"I wondered sometimes while we travelled together. You hung out with Burt and Dusty whom everyone knew were gay. I could never get you to go out with a girl." David chuckled.

"I'm sorry," he apologised.

"What the hell are you apologising for?" David turned to him.

Randy shrugged. "For not telling you. Maybe for not being strong enough to admit out loud what I'd always known."

"Shit, man. Don't be sorry for that. You didn't know how I'd take it and it's safer to stay silent than to say something and end up with your ass whipped." He nodded back towards the restaurant where Les was walking out with David's parents. "He's good for you.

I can see that. I've never seen you so relaxed as you were tonight."

"Les is making me comfortable in my own skin." Randy waved to his lover.

"You heading back out on the circuit?"

"I'll leave tomorrow to get down to Mesquite for the weekend and then figure out where I'm heading after that."

"Why so early? It'll take you two days at the most to get down there." David frowned.

"I don't want to drag it out. I need to start getting used to not having him around all the time. I've got family down in Texas, so I'll stop in and see them for a day." He shook his head. "I'm not as eager to head out as I used to be."

"That's what happens when you find the right one. I've seen it happen to a lot of cowboys. To be honest, I never thought you'd stick it out this long." David took a hit of his cigarette.

"If I had the nerve, I'd quit today and go back to the ranch with Les," he confessed in a low voice.

"I guess you've got to work up to that, but I get the feeling Hardin'll stick with you no matter what." David moved away as Les walked up to them. "Thanks for the offer, Hardin. Dad and I'll talk it over and get back to you tomorrow."

Les shook David's hand. "Great. Here's my card—it's got my cell number on it. Dusty, Burt and I will be on the road with the bulls tomorrow. Take all the time you want. It's an open-ended deal."

Randy gave his friend a slap to his shoulder. "When I stop by Les' ranch, I expect to see you there, working hard."

"We'll find some horses for you to try out when you're home." David nodded and headed over to where his parents were waiting.

"Did you tell him?" Les asked as they climbed in the truck.

"He asked and I told him. There's no point in denying it when he'll be around the ranch a lot. Considering we don't hide when we're there, I didn't want him to be surprised if he found us kissing." Randy took Les' hand and squeezed. "I'm not as ashamed of being gay as I used to be. I'm not proud of it yet, but you can't change a lifetime of hiding overnight."

Les lifted Randy's knuckles to his mouth and kissed them. "You're right, baby, and I'm proud of the steps you've taken so far. Let's get back to the hotel. I plan on taking all night to say goodbye to you."

"Did you have to say that?" He groaned as his cock filled and pressed against the zipper of his jeans.

"I plan on saying and doing a lot of things to you when we get back to the hotel." Les grinned at him.

The tyres might have squealed a little as Randy pulled out of the parking lot, but he wasn't worried about that. He wanted to get back to the hotel to enjoy the man riding beside him.

Chapter Twenty

"Hey, Randy, you heading out today?"

Randy turned to see Tony strolling up to him, carrying his gear bag. The bull rider's eyes were tired, but his bright smile was still there.

"I'm heading to Mesquite. Got family down there I thought I'd visit for a day before the rodeo. Need a lift?"

"Yeah. The guy I usually travel with is taking a couple weeks off. His girlfriend is about to have a baby and he's still trying to convince her to marry him." Tony laughed. "I keep telling him a rodeo cowboy isn't good marriage material, but he won't listen to me."

"Throw your bag in the truck." Randy jerked a thumb to his truck.

Yawning, he stretched. Every muscle in his body ached, but it was a good ache. He and Les had spent more time making love than sleeping the night before. He was going to miss that. He laughed at himself. Yes, he would miss the fucking, but he would also miss the feel of Les' body lying next to him in bed and the sound of the man breathing. Shit. He had it bad.

"Where's Hardin?" Tony leaned on the hood of the truck next to him.

"He's settling the bill for all of us. We're meeting the guys for breakfast. They'll head back to the ranch." He pushed his cowboy hat back on his head and lifted his face to the bright morning sun. The warmth softened the sting at the back of his eyes.

Tony nudged him with a hip. "Cowboy up, kid. If you're riding the circuit, you leave people behind."

Sighing, he nodded. "I know, but it's never been this hard before. Hell, I walked away from my family without a second glance. I mean, I love my sister, but I had to get out before things got worse between my dad and me."

Tony knocked some ash off the cigarette he'd lit. "I left at fifteen because I didn't want to deal with the shit I was getting from all of my family. I don't have one relative who doesn't think I'm a hell-born demon intent on corrupting every good boy's morals." The bull rider's laugh was harsh and bitter. "Total bullshit, man. The guys I fucked in my hometown are so scared of their families—they'll never come out of the closet. They'll be married and have ten children by the time they're forty. However, will they be happy? No, because they'll be living a lie."

"Are you happy?" Randy glanced at the front door of the hotel to check on Les.

"Kid, no one's really happy. I'm not living a lie. I'm as out as I can be at the moment. I wish I could find a guy like you or Les, but, right now, there's a whole bunch of cowboys to choose from. Maybe someday I'll find the right guy and settle down. I've learnt the hard way to make a family with people I want to love." Tony's cheeks turned a little red.

"I think you're starting to insinuate yourself into our family, Romanos, but that's okay. We like you." Randy squeezed the man's shoulder.

Les stepped out of the hotel lobby and Randy straightened. He admired Les' loose-hipped walk as the man strolled over to them. Les was lean and tall, with more of a muscular build than Randy. Margie had explained that Les was still trying to rebuild his body after the injury and strength of body was important in keeping the muscle weakness away. Les wore khaki pants with brown Justin ropers. The blue dress shirt was unbuttoned to reveal a white T-shirt underneath. The brown Stetson's brim was pulled low enough to hide most of the dent in Les' skull. Les' St George's medal rested on top of the T-shirt.

"Hey, Hardin, looking good, as always." Tony greeted Les with a smile and a hug.

"Look what the cat dragged in," Randy joked.

Les hugged Tony back then moved to stand beside Randy. Randy felt a warm hand settle on the small of his back. Relaxing slightly, he leaned a little into his support.

"Are you joining us for breakfast, Tony?" Les shifted closer.

Randy breathed in the comforting scent of the earthy cologne Les had put on that morning. He sighed as Les rubbed the aching muscles in his lower back.

"If you'll let me tag along. I'm catching a ride down to Mesquite with the kid here." Tony nodded at Randy, his eyes gleaming with lust and amusement.

"Why do you call me kid?" Randy asked, then Les' hand sliding down and squeezing his ass distracted him. "Um, I'm sure I'm older than you."

"You might be older than me in years, but I've got you beat in sheer experience." Tony headed around the truck to climb in.

"Just leave him a little innocent, Romanos. I happen to like them young and inexperienced," Les told the bull rider as he pinched Randy's ass.

"Ow," Randy complained, rubbing the abused piece of flesh. "That's not fair. I can't pay you back."

"Now, baby, you know I'll let you do anything you want to me. You just have to be brave enough to do it."

The smirk on Les' face told Randy his lover knew he wouldn't do anything where people could see them. He growled and Les laughed.

Tony leaned out of the window and said, "Come on, guys. There are eggs and bacon calling my name somewhere."

"Tease." Randy slid in behind the wheel.

"That's just one of the things you love about me." Les settled in the seat beside him, spreading those long legs to draw his gaze to the bulge the khaki pants weren't hiding.

"There's at least one other thing I like about you." His voice dropped to a husky whisper. He started to reach over and fondle Les' hard-on.

"Hey, there is someone else in this vehicle with y'all. You should have stayed in bed longer. Jesus." Tony's voice shot through him.

His cheeks burned with embarrassment as he yanked his hand back and turned the truck on. Looking behind him to back up, he caught Tony's eye. The bull rider gave him a smile and a thumbs-up. Relaxing, he should have realised Tony wouldn't be uncomfortable with their flirting.

"I knew we shouldn't have given you a ride," Les groused.

"Oh, excuse me for interrupting the impromptu hand job you were about to get. I hear denying yourself sexual release is good for the soul." Tony snickered as Les shot him a baleful glare.

"So how did you celebrate last night?" Les turned to face forward again.

Tony's dark eyes gleamed and Randy hastened to say, "That might not be information we really want to hear."

"Don't worry, kid. I was good last night. Didn't get into any fights or hit on any cowboys who weren't gay. Did some drinking, some dancing and some fucking. All in all, a pretty good night."

"Fucking? Who?" Randy looked in the rear-view mirror to see Tony shake his head.

"Now, kid, I don't fuck and tell." Tony stared out of the window for a moment. "He's a good guy, but further in the closet than you were. I'm not the man Les is, so I wouldn't be able to prise him out of there."

"Any man in his right mind would never go back in the closet after spending a night with you, I'm sure," Randy reassured the bull rider while shooting a look over at Les.

"Some people fear what people will say more than what the lies will do to their souls," Les commented.

They were silent for the rest of the ride to the restaurant. Dusty and Burt were already there and seated when they walked in.

* * * *

"We should probably get going," Dusty suggested while looking at his watch. "We have to stop by the fairgrounds and pick up the bulls, still."

Les picked up the bill. He stood at the counter to pay for it and watched the guys say goodbye to Randy. He didn't like the idea of Randy leaving him, but he wasn't going to stop the man.

"I'll take care of him for you," Tony said quietly from where the bull rider stood, waiting for him.

"I know you will and I appreciate it." He handed the lady at the register the money. Taking the change, he smiled at her then turned. He reached in his pocket and pulled out a card. "If you end up needing anything, you call me. I'm not sure Randy will. He's used to being on his own and doesn't realise that I'll do anything for him."

"A man has his pride, Hardin." Tony took the card and stuck it in his front pocket.

"I know that, but if it comes down to sleeping in the truck or calling me for hotel money, I hope you'd call."

"I like the comfort of a bed. I'll call." Tony led the way outside then said goodbye to Dusty and Burt. Tipping his hat to Les, he headed to Randy's truck.

"We'll wait in the truck for you, boss." Burt grabbed Dusty's arm and pulled the shorter man away.

"This isn't really a private goodbye, is it?" Les gestured to the restaurant windows and the people watching them.

"It might be a good thing, though, because if I started kissing you, I might not be able to stop." Randy's blue eyes flashed with desire and a little sadness.

"Just think of all the sex we'll have when you get back home," Les murmured.

Randy's cheeks turned beet red and he shifted slightly. "Thanks, Les. Now I have to drive with a hard-on."

Les reached up and took off his St George's medal. He took Randy's hand and placed the necklace in his palm. "Take this. It'll keep you safe while you're riding and travelling."

"I can't take this, Les. This is the only thing you have of your mother's," Randy protested, trying to give it back.

Les closed his fingers around Randy's, trapping the necklace under them. "Keep it. My mom would have wanted you to have it. I can't give you a kiss, but I can give you this. Wear it next to your heart and know I'm thinking of you all the time."

Randy's blue eyes shone with tears. In a move that shocked and surprised Les, Randy rose up on his toes and kissed the corner of his mouth. Backing up, he called, "Thank you. I'll call you when we stop tonight."

He touched his mouth and nodded. Dazed, he watched Randy's truck peel out of the parking lot. He walked over to where Dusty and Burt waited in the ranch truck. Settling in, he threw his hat on the seat next to him and closed his eyes.

"Shit, that kid has more balls than I thought he did," Dusty commented as Burt drove them towards the fairgrounds.

"He's always had balls, Dusty. He just never had any reason to step out of the shadows." Burt's eyes shot back to look at Les in the mirror. "When you know there's someone there to catch you or back you up, you're willing to walk out on a few more limbs."

Les didn't say anything. He wanted to be home already, so he could take Sam for a ride and pout a little because Randy had left.

* * * *

Randy and Tony decided to stop around eight that night. The bull rider had been pleasant company. They had talked about their families and what rodeos they enjoyed riding at. Tony headed off to get them some takeout while Randy checked them in and took their bags to their room.

Throwing the bags on the floor, he flopped on one of the beds and stared up at the ceiling. Les' necklace hit him in the chin. He took it off and held it up so he could look at it. He heard the door open and close, but Tony didn't say anything.

"I have to give it back to him," Randy said without looking at the bull rider.

"Why?" Tony nudged his leg with a foot. "Come and eat."

"Aside from pictures, this is the only thing he has from his mom. She died when he was born." Randy put the necklace on again and moved over to the small hotel table. "I shouldn't have this."

"Again I'm compelled to ask, why?" Tony handed him a couple of burgers and an order of fries.

"This is something very special to him." Randy unwrapped one of the burgers.

Tony sat across from him at the table and studied him. "It's his property to give away. I don't know how much pride he has. Maybe you'll insult him by giving it back." The bull rider's face was serious when he said, "And maybe you're more special to him than a necklace."

Randy shook his head. "I don't believe that's true."

"What's so hard to believe? You're a good-looking man. I mean, if you weren't with Hardin, I'd fuck you."

Blushing, Randy laughed. "I'm not sure if that's a compliment, Tony. Seems to me that you take what you can get."

"Sometimes beggars can't be choosers, kid, but if I found a man like you I'd scoop him up in a heartbeat. Don't do Les a disservice by thinking he doesn't know what he's doing. The man's been through a lot and he's learnt a few things. First would seem to be not to take anything for granted because you never know when it'll all disappear. Second, he knows a good thing when he sees it." Tony sipped his soda and smiled at him. "This is the most important ride of your life, Randy. Ride it as long and as far as it's willing to take you. You never know what you might find when it's over."

They finished their dinner in silence. After he threw the papers in the garbage, Tony grabbed a jacket and headed towards the door.

"Where are you going?" Randy enquired.

"Going to the bar across the street to have a smoke and a beer. When you get done calling Les, you can join me if you want."

Randy was reaching for his phone as the door shut. He'd programmed Les' number in earlier that day. Rolling over on his back, he closed his eyes and waited for someone to answer.

"Hello." Les' deep voice spread over his body like syrup over pancakes.

"Hey," he managed to get over the lump in his throat. Who knew a man's voice could make his cock stand at attention?

"Baby, it's great to hear from you." Les' voice held a smile in it.

He heard a rustle. "Where are you?"

"In bed." Les' voice got lower. "Where are you?"

"Lying on top of the bed in our hotel." He reached down and adjusted his hard-on to find more room in his suddenly too tight pants. "Tony went to the bar. Probably to give me some privacy."

"He's a good guy. I'm glad you took him with you."

Randy unzipped his jeans and stroked his shaft. "Yeah, he is, but I'm glad he's not here right now."

"How much are you missing me?" Les growled.

"I can't tell you," he moaned as he pumped his fist and tightened his grip.

"Are you jerking off while you're talking to me?"

If it hadn't sounded like Les was turned on, he'd be embarrassed. Instead he kept humping his hand and groaning.

"Are you imagining it's my hand on your cock? Squeezing and pumping?" Les' accent got thicker.

"Uh." He could feel his climax begin to build.

"Or are you fucking my ass? Harder, baby. I need to feel you," Les encouraged him.

"Shit," he cried as he came. Wet heat bathed his hand in spurts. Over his own harsh breathing, he heard Les let out a low moan.

"You okay?" he asked when his heartbeat had calmed down.

"I am now." His lover laughed.

"I'll have to make sure to call you late at night. Tony will be having a beer every night." He chuckled.

"Does it sound too sappy to tell you I miss you already?" Les' voice was soft as he spoke.

"Sure, it's sappy, but I like hearing it. I'll be sappy as well. I'm going to miss sharing a bed with you."

"I know what you mean." There was silence on Les' end for a moment.

A door shut in the hotel hallway and Randy remembered Tony. He didn't want to get caught with his dick hanging out.

"I have to clean up before Tony comes back." He was reluctant to say goodbye.

"I'm sticky as well, so I'll tell you sweet dreams. Call me when you can tomorrow."

He heard rustling again and figured Les was climbing out of bed. Sitting up, he wiped his hand on his shirt with a grimace. "I will. We should be stopping around midday." He hesitated for a second. "Sweet dreams, love."

Hanging up before Les could say anything, Randy tossed his phone on the mattress and stood. Part of him was surprised by his choice of endearment, but the other part said it was about damn time. He headed for the shower, thinking it was going to be a long couple of weeks.

Chapter Twenty-One

One month later

"I'm done," Randy announced as he and Tony were packing their bags at the hotel.

"Done?" He saw the bull rider glance at his suitcase and the pile of clothes he still had to fold.

"I don't plan on riding this weekend."

"It's Labor Day weekend, kid. There's rodeos all over the place," Tony commented.

"I know but I want to see Les and I don't care how pathetic that makes me sound." He cringed at the defiant tone in his voice.

The last month had been hard. He'd never missed someone so much and yet he'd never ridden so well. He hadn't won every event he'd entered, but he'd finished in the money every time. The money and points he'd won had put him comfortably in second place in the standings for the World Championship.

"Doesn't sound pathetic. Sounds like you're getting your head on straight." Tony helped him finish packing. "I'll take care of the hotel if you get breakfast."

"Good deal. If we start out after breakfast, we'll be in Cleary by tomorrow morning. If you've entered anywhere, you can take my truck to get there. Just be back with it on Tuesday next week."

Tony threw their bags in the truck. "Do you think Les would mind if I crash at the ranch for the weekend? I've been riding good, but I want to relax for a couple days before we start the serious competitions for the finals."

Randy shrugged. "I doubt he'd mind."

"Thanks." Tony headed back inside to pay the bill.

Now that his decision was made, Randy felt excitement building. He would love to go through a drive-through and get breakfast that way, but he and Tony had established a routine for the Monday after an event. They'd find a good restaurant, sit down and rehash the weekend. Like any good cowboy, he was superstitious and didn't want to screw up a good thing.

Tony climbed into the cab. "Let's find some breakfast and get you back to Hardin before you explode."

He blushed as he pulled away from the hotel. Explode was a good word for how he felt. The need to do more than talk to Les on the phone had built until the pressure was too much. He wanted to look into Les' brown eyes and know he was welcomed.

* * * *

Tony pulled out of the restaurant driveway—he'd agreed to drive part of the way to the ranch.

"You might want to give Hardin a heads-up that we'll be arriving tomorrow," Tony suggested. "You never know if he's got something planned for the weekend."

"He didn't say anything when I talked to him last night." Randy reached for his phone.

"Sure but things change." Tony shot him a glance.

Nodding, he dialled the number.

"Hello, Hardin Farms," Margie's voice came over the phone.

"Hey, Margie," he said.

"Master Randy, how are you doing?" The joy in Margie's voice warmed his heart.

"I'm doing great. Is Les around?" He shifted, bouncing his knee up and down with impatience.

"Master Leslie is out working some of the horses. Would you like me to go get him?"

"No, just have him give me a call when he gets a chance." Disappointment welled in him. He wanted to talk to his lover right then.

"I'm sure he'll be in for lunch. I'll give him the message. Master Leslie tells me you've been doing very well with your riding."

Randy laughed. He knew Margie didn't know anything about rodeo, but she always asked him about it when he called and she answered the phone. "I'm doing really well."

They chatted for a few minutes and then he hung up. "Damn, he wasn't in the house."

"Well, Hardin does manage to do more than the paperwork at the ranch," Tony remarked.

"I know that, dumbass. I was just hoping to be able to tell him right away that I was coming back to the ranch." He turned on the radio. Country music poured out and he settled back to stare out of the window.

"He'll call soon enough." Tony tapped his fingers against the steering wheel in time with the music.

Randy tried to relax, but, for the first time, he realised he was excited about going back to the town where he had grown up. He wasn't going home and never would return to the place he had lived most of his life. He watched the hills and scrubland of Wyoming flash past him and thought about how much Les' ranch was coming to mean home to him.

* * * *

Les stepped into the cool shade of the house and hung his hat up on the hook by the door. He threw his gloves on the stand underneath the hook.

"Margie, I'm going to take a shower before I get lunch. It's getting hotter than hell out there," he called to his housekeeper while making his way through the house.

"Okay. Oh, Master Leslie, Master Randy called a little earlier today. I told him I'd have you call him when you got in." Her voice drifted in from the kitchen.

"Thanks." He detoured to his office. He wondered what Randy wanted. The cowboy usually didn't call him until they were settled for the night. Sitting behind his desk, he ignored the piles of papers to reach for the phone. He swivelled his chair so he could look at the mountains.

"Hey, man," Randy answered.

"Margie told me you called, baby. Is everything all right?" He slouched a little in the chair. His body reacted the way it always did when he heard Randy's voice. His cock got hard and he had to resist the urge to rub it.

"Yeah, everything's great. I just wanted to let you know that Tony and I are heading to the ranch. We'll be there tomorrow morning." There was excitement and a touch of hesitation in his voice.

"No shit? That's great." He sat up, joy rushing through him. He'd been making vague plans to head to whichever rodeo Randy planned on riding at over the weekend, but this was even better.

"I decided I was missing some things on the ranch too much and I don't need the money or the points." Les heard a muffled voice in the background. "Right. Tony wants me to make sure it's okay that he comes and stays at the ranch this weekend as well. He's not riding anywhere either."

A smile broke out on Les' face at the thought of the young bull rider. "The more the merrier, baby." He looked down at his desk and caught a glimpse of a brochure he'd received. It reminded him of a phone call he'd got last night. "You still want to go see a horse show with me?"

He was sure the change in conversation puzzled Randy a little, but Randy said, "Yeah. Are there any over the weekend?"

"There's a big one in the Hamptons on the east coast. I got a call from an old friend inviting me to come and stay at his house during the show. I told him no, since I planned to meet up with you somewhere."

"You were going to do that?" Happiness filled the words.

"Sure, it's been a long time since I've seen your face. I thought I'd hold you at night, among other things," he teased.

An embarrassed laugh came over the phone. "I can just guess what those other things are. If you want to go out east, I'm game. Your friend won't mind me coming with you, will he?"

"No, he knows I have a new partner. We can fly in on Thursday and catch the last three days of competition." He closed his eyes for a moment. "This will be the first event I've attended since my accident," he murmured.

"If you don't want to go, we don't have to, Les." Randy's voice lowered.

"It's okay. It'll be strange not competing but you'll be there and that'll make it easier. I love showjumping. It was part of my life since I can remember and I want that joy back, even if I can't ride."

"We're stopping for lunch now, but I think we're planning on driving straight through, so we'll be there early tomorrow morning."

"Call me when you get close and I'll make sure the door's unlocked." He cleared his throat and said, "I've missed you, Randy."

"I've missed you, too." Randy hung up.

Les hung up slowly and sat for a moment before he picked the phone up to call his friend. He had to let the man know he and Randy would be there on Thursday night then call his pilot. The man needed to file a flight plan and get the plane ready to leave on Thursday. It was time to start living again, and visiting some of his old stomping grounds would help to find closure to his past.

Thirty minutes later, he was done. Margie peeked around the corner of the office door. "I thought you were taking a shower and then having lunch."

"I will, but I called Randy first. He and his travelling companion, Tony, will be arriving early tomorrow morning." He couldn't keep the smile off his face.

"Oh, Master Leslie, that's wonderful news. We'll have to plan a dinner of Master Randy's favourites tomorrow night. I'll get the other guest room ready for his friend."

Her excitement made him laugh. "One would think you are more excited than I am about Randy coming back."

She laughed with him. "He's been good for you, Master Leslie. I haven't seen you so happy in several years." Margie hugged him when he moved to stand beside her.

"You never liked Taylor, did you?" He hugged her back.

Margie bit her lip and shot him a glance, but she didn't say anything.

"Come on, Margie. You can tell me. It's not like I'm ever going to take him back or fire you for telling me how you feel." He crossed his arms and leant back against his desk.

"You're right. I always thought Mr Lourdin picked you because of the horses." She frowned.

"You mean you don't think he would have asked me out if Hardin horses hadn't been so good," he commented.

"I'll be honest and say no, I don't. I think he saw you were young and innocent, so he took advantage of that. Also, it didn't hurt that you were good-looking. That's why I never welcomed him." Margie glared at him as if she expected him to argue with her.

"You're right." He saw her stare at him in surprise. "I had a lot of time to think about everything while I was in the hospital and rehab centre. When I was riding, Taylor had access to the top horses in the country without having to do any sort of work to earn them. When I was injured, there wasn't anyone there to train the horses for him. He panicked when he realised he was going to have to do more than ride. So he bought me out and hired a trainer. That way nothing changed. He still had great horses and someone else was doing the hard stuff. I haven't heard whether he's doing well or not. He never loved me and I've accepted that."

"Master Randy isn't interested in your horses or the ranch. He's into you and that makes me like him." She blushed.

Bending down, he kissed her cheek. "I like him too." He straightened and moved to the door. "I'm taking a shower. Is Lindsay here?"

"No, sir. She went into Cleary. I believe she's trying to find a job." Margie headed back down the hall to the kitchen.

"I wish she knew how to do accounting," he muttered as he went into the bathroom and stripped. Turning on the shower, he grimaced at the thought of all the paperwork waiting for him when he had got done with lunch.

Chapter Twenty-Two

The ringing of the phone woke Les up. Rolling over, he grabbed the receiver.

"Hello," he murmured.

"Hey, Hardin, we've just hit Cleary. We'll be at your ranch in ten minutes." A strange voice filled his ear.

"Who is this?" He sat up and scrubbed a hand over his face. Glancing at the clock, he saw it was five in the morning.

"Sorry. It's Tony. Randy's driving like a bat out of hell to get home as soon as possible." Tony laughed.

"Oh. I'll make sure the door's unlocked." He picked a pair of jeans off the floor and tugged them on.

"Great. We'll be ready to crash for a while when we get there." Tony hung up.

Listening to the dial tone, Les tried to make his brain work. He hated waking up early in the morning—he'd never got used to it on horse show days either. He zipped his jeans, but didn't bother to button them. Making his way to the front door, he popped the lock and stepped outside on the porch. The early morning air held a chill. The brisk breeze was filled with the scent of horses, cattle and hay. He loved that smell and always had. He'd spent hours in the stables at Hardin Stables in Virginia, mucking out stalls and brushing horses. Out here, he couldn't muck out as many as he used to because of his injury, but the horses never looked better than when he'd got done grooming them. Leaning against one of the posts, he stared up at the stars that were beginning to fade in the night sky. He was getting used to how close they looked out here.

He was about to go back inside when Randy's red truck drove into view and pulled to a stop in front of the house. Les wanted to yank Randy out and kiss him until the man couldn't breathe. Instead, he stayed on the porch.

Tony jumped out first. With a wave, the bull rider reached into the bed of the truck and pulled out two bags. Les nodded at him, but his gaze was centred on the dark-haired, blue-eyed cowboy climbing out from behind the wheel.

"Morning." Randy smiled at him.

"Morning, baby." He didn't back up as Randy invaded his space. Reaching out, he cupped the stubble-roughened cheek. "Welcome home."

Randy wrapped strong arms around his waist and pulled him tight to the muscled chest. Their lips crashed together with fierce need. Tongues duelled and stroked. Teeth bit. Les slid his hands up and tangled them in Randy's curls. Tilting Randy's head, he took the kiss even deeper.

Moaning, Randy grabbed his ass and squeezed. Les pressed against the hard bulge in those tight jeans. He wanted to ride that long cock. He'd missed the explosive sex they had—jacking off during phone calls wasn't the same.

"Find a room, you two. Trust me. A bed's more comfortable." Tony's voice was like a bucket of ice.

"Shit." He stepped back reluctantly. "Sorry, man." He gave the bull rider a quick hug.

"Don't apologise. I don't mind but others might not like you screwing on the porch." Tony slapped his shoulder.

"Come on in. I'll show you the guest room Margie got ready for you."

Les led the way through the house. He paused in the kitchen long enough to leave a note for his housekeeper. Stopping outside the first guest room, he gestured to Tony.

"This is your room for as long as you want it." He pointed to the door across the hall. "There's the bathroom. You'll be sharing it with our other guest, so don't wander around naked. Lindsay might not appreciate it."

"I'll try to remember that. See y'all at lunch." Tony disappeared behind his door.

Les and Randy walked to Les' room. As soon as the door shut, they were in each other's arms, kissing and trying to get naked. Randy broke their kiss to strip off his own shirt. Les unbuckled and unsnapped Randy's jeans. Sliding his hand down behind the zipper, he cradled Randy's cock in his hand.

"Dreamed of this," Randy grunted, his lean hips already moving.

"I've dreamed of more than just my hand on your cock, baby." Les gave the shaft a hard squeeze then pulled away.

Randy frowned at him. Grinning, he moved over to the nightstand. Opening a drawer, he took out some lube and condoms.

"Get naked," he ordered.

A minute later, he and Randy were lying on the bed. Hands relearned spots that made the other one groan. Mouths found tender skin to make bodies jerk. Cocks were stroked and pre-cum tasted.

Les had a feeling the first time would be over fast because a month was a long time to do without the man who drove him to distraction.

"Les, gonna," Randy warned.

"Not yet. Want you in me when you come."

He sheathed Randy's cock and slicked him. He prepared himself, since he figured Randy would come just from doing that. Shifting, he settled on his hands and knees.

"Now, baby."

He dropped his head forward and tried to relax as the head of Randy's cock breached his ass. Randy pushed forward slowly, but didn't stop until he was buried deep inside Les. A calloused hand smoothed down his back, trying to ease the pressure.

"Les?"

He heard the question in Randy's voice. Nodding, he braced his hands against the headboard. Randy's first thrust nailed his gland and he cried out.

"Missed this," Randy confessed.

Les' brain wasn't working, so nothing came out of his mouth except noises that meant 'Fuck me', 'Harder', and 'Please'. Randy must have been able to read his mind because that's exactly what the man did. Les' climax built and he knew all it would take was one touch of a hand to his cock to make him come. Before he could do more than think about taking his hand off the headboard, Randy gripped his shaft and squeezed.

"Fuck," he cried as his cock got harder and throbbed.

"That's what I'm doing." Randy's breath burned Les' ear.

"Close," he told his lover.

"I know. Come on my cock, love. I want to feel you milk my dick dry." Randy twisted his fingers around the base of Les' cock, drawing them up and down with quick motions.

Those words were all it took for Les to explode. Strings of cum coated Randy's hand, Les' stomach and the pillows in front of him. His inner muscles closed around the cock deep in him and he milked Randy's own climax from him. One more thrust and Randy filled the condom, biting the muscle at the top of Les' shoulder.

Collapsing on the bed, they cuddled close while their breathing slowed down. Les kissed Randy with gentle lips.

"It's good to have you home, baby." He rubbed a thumb over Randy's plump bottom lip.

"I'll be coming back more often now that I know what kind of welcome is waiting for me." Randy nipped at his thumb.

Les wanted to ask him to stay, but he knew Randy wasn't ready to admit how serious their relationship was. The fact Randy had never used the word 'home' when he spoke of Les' ranch told him the man still didn't believe that Les would stick around and continue to love him. Les knew Randy wasn't going to lay claim to a partner or admit any commitment without knowing he'd always be welcomed. He just kissed Randy again and climbed out of bed.

"Let's get cleaned up and crash for a while. Margie won't bother us. David and his dad aren't supposed to be back until this afternoon." He turned the shower on. "They went to a rough stock auction. Picked up a few mares we might be able to use to start our programme with."

"Well, they have the knowledge to pick out good ones for you." Randy joined him under the water. "Talked to Casey Adams before we left. He's going to give you a call about shipping the bulls to a couple rodeos in September."

"I know Dusty and Burt are getting restless, I'll send them out with the stock again. They picked up three more bulls. Maybe I'll talk to Adams and see if I can send those three out with the others. Start getting them used to the noise and travel." Les scrubbed his body clean.

"Mmm…" was all he got from Randy.

Glancing over his shoulder, he saw his lover leaning against the tiles. The man was half asleep. He grinned and finished washing Randy down. Supporting the tired man, he dried him off and tucked him into bed. Going back into the bathroom, he shut off the water and threw the towels in a basket.

He climbed under the covers and snuggled close to his lover. Brushing a kiss over the nape of Randy's neck, he whispered, "Welcome home, love."

* * * *

Randy woke to find a warm, moist mouth engulfing his cock. He looked down over his stomach. Les' brown eyes shone up at him from where he was sucking on his shaft. Running his hand softly over Les' hair, he smiled down at him.

"Nice wake-up call," he joked.

The chuckle Les gave vibrated along the underside of Randy's cock and he moaned. He arched his hips off the blankets as Les moved up and down, picking up the tempo. Soon he was fucking Les' mouth. A hot hand cupped his balls and rolled them around between strong fingers.

"Les." Randy tightened his hands, holding his lover's head still while he thrust.

Les didn't fight him, just swallowed his cock. Randy might have been embarrassed by the noises he was making, but his attention was trained on the mouth sucking him. When Les' finger slid into his ass, he shouted and came hard enough to see stars. Les sucked him dry then licked him clean. He was trying to get his energy back when his calves were placed over Les' forearms. Hands took hold of his thighs and he found himself being slowly impaled on Les' cock.

Relaxed from his earlier climax, Randy's body took Les in without too much resistance. Their loving was slow and gentle, with none of the fierce urgency it had had when he'd first arrived home. He ran his hands over Les' chest, plucking and twisting the hard nipples. Les' gaze remained focused on his face, as if the man was afraid Randy would disappear.

As the minutes seemed to amble by, Randy's passion began to rise again. Les' strokes grew faster and Randy's words of encouragement filled the air.

"Faster. Right there," he forced out through clenched teeth. His eyes rolled as Les' cock scraped over his gland. "Please."

"Touch yourself." Les' hands held Randy's thighs tight enough to leave bruises.

He started jacking off in tempo to Les' movements. The combination of his hand gripping his cock and Les filling his ass with each thrust of his hips was enough to take him over the edge.

"Love." His voice was harsh and low as his cum shot from his cock in strings of white.

Les slammed into his ass, hard, twice more before Randy saw that grimace of painful pleasure cover his lover's face. Les shuddered and jerked as he filled the condom. Letting go of his legs, Les collapsed on him. He wrapped his arms around Les' broad shoulders, running his hands up and down Les' sweat-covered back.

"Can't get this type of fucking on the circuit," he murmured.

"I should hope not." Les sounded indignant, but Randy couldn't see the man's face. Les had it buried in the pillow next to Randy's head. "Were you looking for it?"

He laughed. "Not this time. Before I met you, I was." Randy brushed a kiss over the ear closest to him.

A door slammed somewhere in the house. He found he was too relaxed to care if anyone knew what he and Les had been doing. A knock sounded on the bedroom door.

"Yes," Les called as he rolled away from Randy.

"The Prestons are back." Jackson's voice drifted through the door.

"Thanks. I'll be out in a few minutes." Les gave a slight groan as he climbed out of bed.

"Hersch, you'd better call your sister and let her know you're back. I don't want to be the one she bitches at when she finds out you're here and I didn't tell her," Jackson said.

"I will," he promised as he made his way to the shower.

Chapter Twenty-Three

Les walked into the dining room with Randy right behind him. Tee and David were chatting with Jackson while they seemed to be thoroughly enjoying Margie's sandwiches. He shook the elder Preston's hand.

"Good to see you back. Think you got some bucking horses?"

"These mares are from quality bloodlines. They've been out on the circuit. Scored high. I thought we'd buck them for a while longer then breed them." Tee smiled at Randy. "Nice to see you again, Randy."

"Mr Preston," Randy greeted him and David. "Les told me you were on a buying trip. Bring back anything I can try?"

"Didn't know you'd be back this week. I figured you'd go on to some of the bigger rodeos." David shot Les' lover a curious glance.

Randy shrugged and sat down. "Don't need the money or the points. I'm still a little sore from the wreck, so I thought I'd rest up."

"And I let him drag my sorry ass here," Tony announced as he strolled in.

Introductions went around and they settled down to lunch, talking business and rodeo in between bites. Les enjoyed the times he got to interact with these cowboys. They were a different breed from the people he had dealt with before. More polite and more honest. When they shook his hand, they looked him directly in the eye. Though they tended to be portrayed as homophobic bastards, the ones he'd met were far more accepting of his choices than most city dwellers. They were God-fearing folks, but they brought a live-and-let-live philosophy to their lives. As long as what he did didn't hurt any of them, they didn't care.

After they had finished lunch, they cleared the table and headed out of the door. Les smiled when Randy patted his hip as he walked past him. Grabbing his hat from its hook, he started out on the porch.

"Master Leslie," Margie called out. "There's a phone call for you."

"Hey, guys, I'll catch up. Have to answer the phone."

The others waved as they made their way to the rough stock barn. Pushing his hat back, Les picked up the receiver.

"Hardin." He watched Randy's tight jean-covered ass walk away from him. He swallowed back a moan. His cock filled and he adjusted his own jeans to find some more room.

"Mr Hardin, this is Peter Skinner. I was wondering if the job offer was still open?" Peter's voice was hesitant and nervous.

"Oh, hell yes, it is. Are you willing to come and try it out?" A jump of excitement raced through him. He hated doing the paperwork for the ranch. He had taken over the reins of his father's corporation after the man's death and those businesses had their own accountants—the ranch and the businesses he'd started out here didn't. He didn't have a good grasp on numbers but he knew how to hire the right people to keep the companies profitable.

"Try it out?" Peter sounded puzzled.

"I don't want you to think you'll be trapped into this job. Give it a try. If you don't like it, I can probably find you a different type of job in one of my companies back east." Glancing out of the window, he saw David and the others leading three large mares to the bucking arena. *Randy must be trying them out,* he thought.

"Okay. I'm willing to do that. When can I start?" Peter's voice held eagerness now.

"How soon can you be here?" Les laughed. "If there's one thing I hate, it's paperwork and crunching numbers."

"I could come over tomorrow."

"Good enough. Come over early. We'll have breakfast and I'll get you up to speed on the accounts."

"Thanks, Mr Hardin. I appreciate this."

"No problem, Skinner. You're a godsend." He said goodbye and hung up. "Margie." He went into the kitchen.

His housekeeper was filling the dishwasher. "That was good news, I hope."

"The best news so far. Peter Skinner will be joining us for breakfast tomorrow. He's going to try out being my accountant for the ranch and the businesses I started out here. Keep your fingers crossed that he doesn't run screaming after seeing the way I've messed things up." He took his hat off and brushed his hand through his hair. Setting his hat back on his head, he winked at her. "We're adding one more stray. Think we have enough room?"

"If not, we can add on to the house. There'll always be room in your heart for those who need help, Master Leslie." She smiled at him. "Now get out there. I know you are dying to see those horses the Prestons brought back for you."

* * * *

Randy looked up as Les approached the arena fence. Those blue eyes sparkled with happiness and—Les hoped—contentment.

"Nothing important?" Randy had got his rigging out of the truck and was checking it over.

"Peter Skinner is taking me up on the offer of a job. Must have gotten fed up working for his grandfather. He'll be over tomorrow morning so I can go over the accounts and paperwork with him." Les leaned in and took a deep breath full of horse, leather oil and man. He nipped Randy's ear before he moved back.

Randy shot him a smouldering glance. "I wish you didn't do that."

Chuckling, he fondled Randy's ass as he bent down to pick up his chaps off the ground. Randy pushed back into his hand and moaned under his breath.

"Okay, you two. Quit that. Randy, get your ass out of his hand and over here. This mare is ready to go," Tony yelled from the bucking chutes.

Randy blushed, but pressed a quick kiss to Les' cheek. "You make me forget where we're at."

Les swatted that tight little cowboy ass as Randy strolled off to where the others were waiting. He made a mental note to try to keep his hands to himself as much as possible while they were outside. His ranch hands were pretty tolerant, but he didn't want to rub their faces in his sexual choices.

"Boss?" Larry, one of his hands, came up to him.

"Yeah, Larry." He kept one eye on the crowd around the horse.

"Do you have a moment to come and check out that little colt horse?"

That got his attention. "Is there something wrong with him?"

"Not exactly. Just come and check him out." Larry had a slight smile on his face, so Les wasn't panicking yet.

"Randy," he called out. His lover looked up from the top of the chutes. "Try them out, then talk to David and Tee about what we should be doing."

Randy waved his hand to let him know he'd heard the order. Les made his way to the small barn where he had housed Sally Jane and her blind colt a couple of months ago. He looked in on them often, since Sam was in the same barn. The colt had grown more confident and explored its paddock without too much trouble, but it still had problems walking on those crooked legs.

Larry didn't take him inside. The hand led him up to the fence and pointed out into the paddock. The foal was standing on shaky legs with its nose buried in the sweet grass his mother was eating. The clank of the bucking gate being pulled caused his head to shoot up and he took off for a few wobbly strides. It wasn't very far or very fast, but the colt ran and Les knew things would be okay for the young horse. It would still take time for those legs to straighten out more and they might never be totally perfect, but he would be able to run and walk.

With a smile, he slapped Larry on the back. "Thanks for showing me, Larry. That's a wonderful sight."

"I thought so, boss. Only what do we do with him when it's time to wean him?" Larry looked worried.

"Let him stay in this barn and, when it's time to put him out, put him in with Sam. The gelding won't mind and it'll keep the little one company. I'm not sure we'll ever be able to put him in with the other horses, but Sam's a good guy. He won't pick on him too much."

"Good idea."

A shout from the arena caught Les' ears. "I've got to get back and make sure none of them kill themselves. You're doing good work, Larry."

He rounded the corner of the barn to see Randy go sailing off the back of the second horse. Tee was on the pick-up horse and he herded the mare into the holding pen. Les wanted to rush out and make sure Randy was okay, but he stayed on his side of the fence. Randy stood up slowly, dusting off his chaps. Les caught the man's blue eyes and he knew his worry showed in his gaze. Randy grinned and gave him a thumbs-up.

"Y'all need to keep that bitch if she can throw Randy two seconds out," Tony joked.

"Hey, big bad bull rider, why don't you get your ass on one of these horses?" Randy reached up and smacked Tony on the ass with his hat.

"Don't have the right gear." Tony grabbed Randy's hat and hit him back with it.

"Not good enough, man. You can borrow mine."

Les watched as his lover hooked a hand around Tony's ankle and pulled the bull rider off the fence.

Landing face-first in the dirt, Tony managed to get a hold of Randy and soon the two of them were rolling around on the ground. Les made sure there weren't any punches being thrown then just let them have fun. The other men gathered around and cheered them on.

"I've never seen him so happy."

Les turned to see Tammy standing next to him. "Jackson call you?"

She shot him a puzzled glance before looking back at the wrestlers. "No. I came over to visit Lindsay. I don't remember hearing him laugh like that since Momma died."

"Sometimes it takes someone a while to get comfortable in his own skin." He thought about his own life. "I knew I was gay when I was seventeen and my dad accepted me, but it took me a long time after that to feel good about who and what I was."

"Daddy never allowed him that chance." Tammy's eyes were sad.

"Now don't cry, girl. Randy's here and he's fine. No use crying for what's happened before." Les tilted her chin up and brushed a tear off her cheek.

"Tammy, stay away from him. Gosh, you've already got one good-looking man. Do you need to start flirting with mine?" Randy shouted from where he'd pinned Tony to the dirt.

Les froze in surprise when Tammy threw her arms around him and hugged him tight. "Thank you so much for bringing my brother back." She gave him a big kiss on the lips. Turning to Randy, she stuck out her tongue. "Maybe he's looking for someone who can stick a horse better than you."

Hoots and hollers were heard as Randy jumped to his feet and chased after his sister. Tammy finally took refuge behind Jackson.

"Save me. He's going to hurt me." Tammy huddled behind Jackson.

Randy sauntered up to the couple. "Now, come on, Jackson. I called you good-looking. Doesn't that win me brownie points?" He turned to reach around the man but Jackson blocked his hand.

"Maybe if I swung that way it would. But I'm not overly keen on having guys call me good-looking." Jackson frowned good-naturedly.

Randy patted the man's chest with a firm hand. "Don't worry. I won't risk tempting you to the dark side. I don't want to make the boss jealous." Randy winked at Les.

While Tammy was distracting Randy, Tony had recovered and gathered a bucket of ice-cold water from the hose. The bull rider sneaked up on Randy, gesturing for Jackson to get out of the way. With casual indifference, Jackson backed away, trying not to alert Randy to what was coming.

"Gotcha," Tony cried as he poured the bucket over Randy's head.

"Holy shit, that's fucking cold," Randy burst out as water dripped from his nose and chin.

Leaning against the fence post, Les could barely catch his breath. His howls of laughter joined the others. Wiping his wet hair off his forehead, Randy pinned him with a glare.

"You didn't even warn me. Where's the loyalty?" Randy stalked towards him.

"Oh, but you know how I like to see you wet," Les stuttered between chuckles.

"TMI, boss," Dusty warned.

Randy walked right up to him, pressing him back against the post. Their chests rubbed together and Les could feel his shirt soaking up the water still dripping from Randy.

He leaned in and whispered, "I'd suggest you strip so I could dry you off properly, but I don't think the others would want to see that."

"Just remember, you're going to be punished for this." Randy stepped back and whirled to point at Tony who was bent over, holding his sides. "Remember paybacks are hell, asshole."

"Playtime's over, boys. Let's get a look at this third mare." Les corralled the men and got them back on track.

Randy's hat had fallen off while he and Tony had wrestled. He picked it up and knocked the dirt off it. Starting to settle it back on his head, he got a good look at the mare David and Tee had run up into the chute.

"Damn," he swore in a low voice.

Les was close enough to hear. "What's the problem?"

"That's the bitch that put me in the hospital three months ago." The cowboy hat went firmly on his head and he walked to the chute.

"You don't have to ride her." Les followed, putting a hand on his shoulder.

"I have to ride her. Can't let one bad spill off her destroy my confidence. I don't have a problem with any of the other horses but what if she's the one I have to ride for the World Championship buckle? Don't want to throw that away because she makes me nervous." Randy stood on the other side of the metal gate and stared the large roan mare in the eye. "What are you calling her now?"

"Hardin Farms Delia."

He shot a look at David. His friend shrugged. "It seemed fitting."

Delia was a rogue horse. Most bucking horses were the type to do the job and when the cowboy got off they'd leave him alone. Delia went after him. She'd go after the pick-up man and his horse as well. There was a demon burning deep inside the mare and she hated men with a passion—Randy could see the rage in her rolling brown eyes. The interesting thing was that the demon didn't take a hold of her until she was put in a chute with a strap around her flanks. As long as she was in an arena, she'd try to hurt anyone or thing in her way. Maybe it was the feeling of being trapped or imprisoned that drove her mad. Lunging in the chute, the mare kicked her feet against the wood and metal.

"Easy, girl. It's okay. It'll be over soon."

Les' voice came from beside him and Randy watched as the roan began to calm down. Her ears swivelled to catch the low honey drawl of Les' voice. He stopped his lover from putting his hand on the mare.

"Last man tried to pet her while she was in the chute almost lost two fingers. Doctors managed to save them, but he'll never be able to bend them again." Randy scaled the gate and climbed over to where David was waiting.

While they put his rig on the mare, he paid attention to the way the mare stood almost as if she were straining to hear Les. David saw him watching and nodded towards Les and the mare.

"She's a wicked bitch, but he's got her eating out of his hand. I've never seen it this easy to get her ready," David commented in a soft voice, trying not to distract the mare.

"I know. I'm almost afraid to get on her." He straddled the chute and eased down on her.

Delia's muscles tensed but she didn't move, except to edge closer to the gate. Randy motioned for Les to get out of the way. Pushing his hat down tight to ensure that it didn't fly off, he wedged his gloved hand into the grip and leant back. He set his feet on Delia's shoulders and took a deep breath. He nodded as he let the air out.

The gate flew open and Delia fired out of there like she'd been shot. The big roan crow-hopped across the arena, trying to jerk Randy's hand out. When he figured out the pattern to her jumping, he started spurring, bringing his spurs to her withers and back down to her shoulders. He held his free hand up and out, working on keeping his balance without touching the horse. It seemed as if, once Delia realised he'd figured out her rhythm, she changed it up. She started bucking hard and fast. The strength in her lunges threatened to whip him forward. He could feel the pressure on his arm and the force that was causing his head to whip around.

He lost all connection with the world around him. His focus centred on him and Delia for what seemed longer than eight seconds. A flash of grey turned his head and he saw Tee riding next to him on the pick-up horse. He managed to work his hand free then jumped onto the rump of Tee's horse.

After he slid off and made his way to the fence, Tee caught up with Delia and undid the flank strap. She stopped bucking but she made a beeline across the arena. Randy's heart jumped into his throat when he saw the mare heading straight for Les. Everyone started yelling for Les to climb the fence. There wasn't time. Delia was moving too fast. Randy closed his eyes. He couldn't watch Les being crushed by that roan body.

"Holy fuck, kid." Tony's voice sounded full of shock.

Opening his eyes, Randy had to blink them again to make sure he was actually seeing what was happening in front of him. Delia hadn't run Les down. The mare was nuzzling Les' chest and it seemed she was trying to get as close to him as possible. Les ran his hands over her neck and mane. David and Tee let their boss take Randy's bucking rig off the mare. Les led Delia over to the holding pen where the other two horses were. He shooed her through the gate, but she was reluctant to go.

Randy chuckled. "I know that feeling, girl," he spoke softly to himself.

Les got her put away without any help from the others. His lover shot a look over at him as if to make sure he was okay. David threw him his rigging.

"Let's go talk about the mares," Randy said as he climbed down off the fence.

Les joined them and they headed to the house.

Chapter Twenty-Four

Two days later in the Hamptons on Long Island, NY

Randy tugged at the bow tie around his neck. Damn, if he had known he was going to have to dress up like a penguin over the weekend, he might have changed his mind. Les had been apologetic about it, though.

They had landed at JFK airport in Les' private jet. Shit, a private jet. Had he missed the part where Les had told him he was a multi-millionaire? He must have, because, when he'd seen the aeroplane, he knew his mouth had flopped opened like a landed fish. They had got off the plane and been driven into Manhattan, where Les had bought him a tuxedo. When the hell was he ever going to wear the thing again?

"When I called to tell Frank where we were, he remembered to tell me that he and his wife were having a charity black-tie dinner tonight. I have a tux already, but we need to get you one." Les had cupped his cheek and stared into his eyes. "I'm sorry. If I had known, I would have suggested we stay somewhere else for the weekend."

He'd shrugged and told his lover it was okay. What could he have said? He had wanted to see the world Les had lived in before coming out west. Little did he know Les was considered a prince in this world.

So he stood, hiding behind a potted plant and trying to find where Les had gone. The minute they had appeared downstairs before this party started, their host had grabbed Les and dragged him off. Randy sipped his whisky and wondered how long he had to stay downstairs.

"Young man, I was wondering if you could help me out." A garrulous voice came from behind him.

Turning, he found a petite, elderly woman leaning on a cane. "Certainly, ma'am. What do you need me to do?"

"Can you escort me out into the garden?" She gestured a trembling hand towards the large French doors that opened out onto a stone patio.

He glanced around to see if he could find Les. Several dark-haired men filled the room, but none of them had the distinctive white streak of Les' hair. "I'll be happy to escort you, ma'am."

"Quit the ma'am crap. I'm sure your mother raised you to be respectful to your elders, but I hate being reminded how old I am. Call me Ethel." The lady might have been old and frail, but Randy could hear her strength in her voice.

"Of course, ma'am. I mean Ethel," he quickly corrected himself when she glared at him.

They made their way along the edge of the crowd. Randy did his best to use his body to block Ethel from the crush of the people. Stepping out onto the stone patio, he took a deep breath of the clean air.

"I hate these things. Too many people. Too much wine. Too many candles. You would think, at my age, I'd know better than to come." Ethel pointed an elegant finger down one of the paths. "Let's take this one and go to the gazebo. I have an urge to stay away for a while. We won't miss anything important."

He gave her his arm to lean on, but he let her lead. They moved into the dark. The farther away from the mansion they got, the better he felt. Taking off his jacket, he spread it out on one of the stone benches so Ethel could sit without getting her dress dirty. After she was settled, he leaned against one of the pillars and stared back at the enormous house they'd left.

"It's a little over the top, isn't it?" Ethel grimaced. "Frank's father always had to show how much money he had."

"You know Frank, then," he asked, more to make conversation than because he really wanted to know.

"Young man, I probably know everyone's family in that house except for yours. I don't remember ever seeing you here before and I've got an eye for a good-looking man."

He couldn't believe he'd blushed because an elderly lady had called him good-looking. "I'm Randy Hersch, Ethel. It's nice meeting you."

"Hersch? I don't remember that name."

He could tell she was trying to place his family in her encyclopaedia of old families. "You wouldn't. I'm from Wyoming."

"Ah. Whom do you belong to then?"

"Belong to?" He didn't appreciate being made to sound as if he were a dog.

"That did make you sound like a slave, didn't it? I meant whom did you come with?" Ethel opened her small purse and pulled out a pack of cigarettes. She tapped one out, but her shaking hands made it impossible for her to light it.

He joined her on the bench and lit it for her. After blowing her first puff away from him, she studied his face for a moment.

"I can't imagine you with any of them in there. They're a thriftless, selfish lot. More interested in getting their names in the paper than actually helping anyone." She leaned over to him as if to confide a secret. "You're the only one in there with a real tan. That's why I chose you."

"That's because I'm a real cowboy, Ethel. I'm here with Leslie Hardin."

"Les is here? I didn't see him in there. We'll have to find him when I'm finished with my cigarette. It's about time that boy came back. Just because Taylor was a total ass doesn't mean he needed to exile himself." The ashes from her cigarette fell to her skirt.

"Maybe he felt he needed time to come to terms with not being able to ride anymore, plus the loss of his father and lover at the same time. How do you know Les?"

"His grandmother on his father's side and I were best friends. I remember Les playing in the garden of my house when he would visit with his grandmother. Such a handsome man." She sighed. "How did you meet?"

He didn't feel as if he needed to hide from her. Her curiosity seemed friendly, not nosy. "The ranch he owns out in Wyoming runs along my father's land. I met him when I came back to visit after an injury sidelined me off the rodeo circuit for a while."

"Rodeo circuit? You are a real cowboy. Do you ride bulls?"

He laughed. "I'm not that crazy. I ride bareback broncs. One of them stomped me pretty good and I had an urge to see my sister."

"Not your father?"

"No. My dad and I aren't really on speaking terms. He's never been a loving father and, once I figured out I was gay, he found a hundred ways to make my life hell. So I don't go back very often."

"No one can hurt us as deeply as those we love." Ethel's wisdom shone in her eyes.

"Well, Dad and I had a disagreement over something and I was heading out of town. I stopped by Les' to check out his horses and ended up staying for a month while I healed."

"The Hardin men have a way of opening their arms and creating a shelter around you so the world can't hurt you until you're strong enough to deal with it again." She took another drag on her cigarette.

"I went back on the circuit last month. Got tired and needed some time to rest. I called up Les and asked if I could come for a visit. So here we are." He flung his arm out to encompass the entire garden.

"Poor man. You must feel like you've fallen down the rabbit's hole. No one's going to talk to you because they don't know if it will win them popularity points, and I think you'd be able to see the ones full of bullshit coming." She patted his hand.

"I told Les I didn't have a problem coming here. I wanted to see what used to be so important to him. He still lights up when he talks about the shows and riding." He smiled at her.

"Ah, yes, Les loved jumping. He went to the Olympics once, before he got Sam. Didn't win anything, but he didn't mind. Winning was never important to him. It was competing against other riders and finding out what his horse could do. He loved the training side of the sport. I know there are quite a few people who would like to have him back here, if only to train their horses for them." She shot him a glance and then looked at the house. "If you're out there, though, I don't see Les coming back here."

"Aunt Ethel, what kind of lies are you telling Randy?" Les' voice came out of the darkness.

Randy watched his lover materialise from the shadows surrounding the gazebo. The black tuxedo fit Les to perfection, emphasising his broad shoulders and trim waist. It made the white streak in his dark hair look distinguished. Randy stood and went to him, not thinking about Ethel or what she'd think. He cupped Les' smooth cheek and brought their lips together in a gentle kiss. They broke apart when Ethel shifted and snuffed out her cigarette.

"Sorry," he apologised to her.

"Don't be sorry. It's rare to see true displays of affection nowadays. Come greet me, you ruffian." Ethel held out her hands to Les.

Pride tugged at Randy's heart when Les knelt in front of the elderly lady and kissed her cheeks with true affection.

"How have you been, Aunt Ethel?" Les sat down next to her.

Randy moved to lean against one of the stone pillars, within easy touching distance of Les.

"I'll admit I've felt better, but I can't complain, young man. Have you recovered fully from your injuries?" A trembling hand reached out and stroked wrinkled fingers through the white streak.

"I have a little weakness on my left side when I overdo things, but, other than that, I'm healthy." Les didn't move away from her.

"Ah, health is good, but what about your heart, Leslie? Has that healed as well?" Ethel glanced between them.

"You're going to embarrass Randy, Aunt. He's not used to talking about things like this as openly as we do," Les dodged.

Randy wondered if his lover really did believe he'd be uncomfortable with the topic or if he just didn't want to talk about it.

"He seemed to be doing just fine before you arrived." Aunt Ethel wasn't going to let him off the hook.

"Yes, my heart is healed. It started healing while I was in rehab and totally recovered two months ago." Les met his eyes and he could see the truth in those brown depths.

"Good for you. Taylor Lourdin wasn't the right one for you. He never really loved you." Ethel started to take another cigarette out of her pack.

"I think one of those is enough for you right now, Aunt." Les went to take it from her.

She glared at him. "Young man, I am eighty years old. I'll die eventually but I don't think I'll die in the next minute from having another cigarette." She looked at Randy. "Can you light this?"

Randy took her lighter and lit the smoke for her. As far as he was concerned, she was right. Death would come for all of them, so why not enjoy some of the simple pleasures before it did?

"You always were good at getting men to do things for you," Les joked. His lover's eyes narrowed as the man studied the elderly woman beside him. "First Margie, now you. If no one liked Taylor, why didn't anyone tell me?"

"At first you were so infatuated with him. I think we all thought it was just puppy love or a first crush. Then you fell in love with him and we knew you wouldn't listen to us if we told you how we felt about him. I hoped you'd learn about his true self without too much pain, but it wasn't meant to be." One of those trembling hands touched Les' chest, right over his heart.

"Maybe all the bad stuff helps me appreciate what I've got now." Les smiled up at Randy.

Randy moved over and put his hand on Les' shoulder. He needed to touch Les, to prove to him that, no matter what, Randy would be there for him. Les' hand came up and closed around his. They stayed like that for a while and for the first time in a long time Randy felt a connection with someone other than his sister.

A discreet cough caused them to look up. A young woman stood just outside the gazebo, her smile slightly embarrassed.

"Sorry to interrupt, Grandmother. Mother sent me out to look for you." Ethel's granddaughter shook her head when she saw the elderly woman snuff out her second cigarette. "You know, Mother will have a fit if she finds out you snuck out of the party to smoke."

"Then we won't tell her," Ethel commanded as she stood and shook out her skirt. Turning, she held out her hand to Randy. "It was wonderful to meet you, Randy. I know you're the right one for Leslie."

Randy took her hand, but, on impulse, he leant down and brushed a kiss over the tissue-paper-thin skin. "Thank you, Ethel. It means a lot coming from you."

"Give me a hug, Leslie. Next time you're in New York, you had better come and visit me. No more hiding."

Les hugged the woman gently. Standing next to each other, they watched the elderly lady and her young granddaughter walk down the path to the house. Randy went to pick up his coat. He brushed the dirt off and would have put it on but Les stopped him.

"Will you dance with me?"

Les' hand settled on his hip. Randy turned into his lover's arms and wrapped his own around Les' neck. It didn't matter that the music didn't reach the gazebo—staring into Les' brown eyes, Randy could almost hear the croon of a slow country song. One of Les' hands cupped his ass and the other worked its way under his shirt to trace gentle patterns along the small of his back.

They moved in small circles, perfectly matched in this as they were in everything else they did together. Letting Les lead, Randy rested his head under Les' chin and listened to his lover's heartbeat. He closed his eyes and allowed the world to slip away. He forgot about everything except how he felt pressed tight against Les.

The passion burning between them simmered for a while. He enjoyed the slow swelling of his cock as their groins brushed together. He savoured the feel of Les' erection rubbing against his. Tilting his head, he placed his lips on the tender skin at the base of Les' throat. He sucked and licked, fighting the urge to mark the man as his.

A low moan came from the throat he tasted. Les' grip on his ass tightened and the fingers on his lower back slid down to tease the top of his crease. He nipped the thin skin over Les' racing pulse. They moved a little faster, the friction from their clothes stoking the fire between them.

He didn't realise Les had a spot picked out until his back ran into one of the stone pillars. Les' shoulders kept his upper body pinned, but both of his lover's hands were fumbling with the buttons on his pants. When Les swore under his breath, Randy laughed.

"We should have asked for Velcro, huh?" He ran his hands over Les' hair and down his back.

Les grunted with satisfaction when the button and zipper yielded to him. Randy sighed into Les' mouth when his warm hand cupped his cock. Their tongues duelled and Les worked his shaft with fast strokes. The coolness of the stone caused him to shiver as his pants were pushed down to give Les better access to his ass and cock. Need flushed his skin and he leaned his head back against the pillar. Les played along his crease, stopping to tap at his hole then moving on to skim over the sensitive skin right behind his balls.

"Les, I'm going to come," he whispered as his balls tightened and his climax pooled at the base of his spine.

"Go ahead. There's no one here but us, baby." Les placed a finger against Randy's lips.

He sucked it in and laved it with his tongue, getting it wet. Pulling it out, Les reached around behind Randy and slid the wet digit into Randy's hole. His cry was smothered by Les' mouth. He found his mind almost overwhelmed by sensations. The strong grip of Les' hand on his cock mingled with the fullness of his ass when Les slipped two fingers in on the next thrust. One bump against his gland and he was coming with a low groan. Les kept pumping until Randy seemed to empty all of his cum.

Randy rested his head on Les' chest and sighed. Arms wrapped him in a cocoon of warmth while he tried to calm his racing heart and catch his breath. He felt Les' erection brush his thigh.

"I might be able to take care of that for you when I catch my breath." He pressed his hand against the bulge.

Les shook his head and stepped back. Handing him a large white handkerchief, Les said, "Clean up and we'll head inside."

Randy looked down at the wet stains on his pants and shirt. "I hope you don't really believe I'm going to go back to the party looking like this."

Les chuckled. "No, I don't. I know a way we can get back inside without dealing with any of that crowd. No one will see us." His lover brushed a kiss over his lips. "I'll let you take care of my problem when we get somewhere with a soft bed."

"Oh, I see," he grumbled while he cleaned up and fastened his pants back up. "The reason you jerked me off out here is because I'm not as old as you. I can take rubbing my ass up against a stone pillar. I think I have some kind of burn back there." He grimaced ruefully.

"Well, being older does have its privileges. One is getting fucked in a soft bed instead of over a stone bench. My knees don't bend as well as they used to. Also, I have a little more control and don't come with the slightest touch to my cock."

Randy glared at Les who winked at him. He threw the piece of material back at Les and grabbed his coat. He started to walk back to the house.

"I also knew you'd be able to get it up sooner than I could and I'm really looking forward to you taking me," Les called.

Randy felt his cheeks heat. *Hope no one is nearby,* he thought. Turning, he gestured for Les to hurry up. "If you want my cock that bad, old man, you better show me how to sneak back inside the house."

Joining him, Les encircled his waist with one arm and took his other hand, holding it to the hard-on under Les' zipper.

"I always want your cock," Les whispered against his lips then pulled him back towards the house.

Randy knew he wore a silly grin, but it was hard not to be happy when he'd just come and had the possibility of coming at least once more before the night was over.

Chapter Twenty-Five

Les strolled into the stall area at the Hampton Classic Horse Show. He took a deep breath and filled his lungs with the smell of leather, horses and hay. It was Sunday and the excitement was at a fever pitch. The participants in the most prestigious class of the week were getting ready to go over to the arena for a walk-through. He stopped at one of the stalls and Randy ran into him.

"Hey, baby, are you okay?" He turned to put a hand on Randy's arm, steadying him.

"Yeah. Sorry, I wasn't watching where we were heading." Randy's eyes were wide and he stared at the horses. "These are some beautiful animals, Les."

Les stroked the nose of the grey horse in the stall in front of him. "Yes, they are. These represent some of the best showjumpers in the world. You're looking at horses that could cost anywhere up to one million dollars apiece."

"No shit?" Randy didn't try to touch the horse, even though the young animal was practically begging for him to pet his nose. "I know Black Bart is worth half that much. I don't think I've ever seen a horse worth a million."

"When he was still competing, Whiskey Sam was worth that. Or, at least, I was offered that much for him."

"Hey, get away from there," a voice called out.

Les turned to see a man about Randy's age come striding up to them. He was dressed in a black riding jacket, tan breeches and black riding boots.

"Edward Monterrose, you've grown up some since I saw you last." Les held out his hand.

"Holy fuck, Leslie Hardin. What the hell are you doing here, man?" The man ignored the hand and gave Les a hard hug.

"Thought I'd come back to the old stomping ground." Les relaxed as Randy rubbed his back in a quick touch. "Just wanted to show my partner here what I used to do for a living."

Edward nodded at Randy. "Nice to meet you. I'm Edward Monterrose. Hardin used to be my riding instructor. Helped me find some good horses as well."

"I'm Randy Hersch." Randy gave the man a shy smile.

"Better keep that one away from the girls. They'll love him," Edward teased. He gestured to the horse. "So you were admiring Gypsy's Salt Mine, huh?"

"I've seen some really great Quarter horses, but I've never seen anything that exudes power like these horses here," Randy spoke up, standing in front of the stall next to Edward's horse.

"What you see around you is a ragtag collection of thoroughbreds, Warmbloods and various mixtures of those two breeds. Not all of them were bred to jump. Some were bred to race, but found out that racing didn't agree with them. Now they're jumping."

Edward patted Gypsy's nose. "This guy's bloodlines say he should excel at dressage, but he couldn't stand it. He wants speed and jumps."

"Who'd you get him from?" Les asked.

"Hey, Edward, if you want to walk the course, you better get out there," one of the other riders warned Edward as they walked past them.

"Shit. I have to go. Would you like to walk the course with me, Les?" Edward glanced at Randy. "I can only take one other person out there with me. You can wait at the in-gate for us."

"I can do that." Randy followed them to the break in the fence where the riders and horses entered the arena.

Les squeezed his lover's hand and headed out on the course with Edward. He studied the jumps and felt the familiar wave of awe at the height and width of the fences.

"So how are you and Gypsy doing?" He and Edward walked to the first fence.

Edward shrugged. "Not too bad. It's his first full year on the circuit, so I'm not expecting great things from him. He's still learning." His friend shot him a glance. "I have to tell you, man, Lourdin had him last year and the bastard almost ruined him. I'm sorry to tell you this, Hardin, but your ex-partner has run your stable into the ground. He can't train worth shit. It was pretty much the year after you retired that everyone began to realise that Lourdin might be a good rider, but you were the real force behind Hardin Stables."

A twinge of remorse ran through Les' heart. He was sad to hear that the stables he and his father had given so much of their lives to were going under. "I'm sorry to hear that," he murmured.

Stopping, Edward stepped close to him and lowered his voice. "I want to warn you, Lourdin's around here. Expect to see him once he hears you're back. And expect him to do what he does best. He'll try to manipulate you into coming back and taking over all the work again, so he can go back to being the golden boy."

Les couldn't help but wonder what it would be like to return to showjumping. For the first twenty-five years of his life, jumping had been his passion. Training horses to do what he loved was just as big a thrill. A voice whispered in his mind, *You can show Taylor how much he needs you and prove to him how wrong he was.*

Randy's baritone laugh ran out over the arena. Les looked back to find his lover kneeling in the dirt, getting his face licked by a puppy. A little girl stood beside him with a happy smile on her face. It was a position Taylor wouldn't be caught dead in. Getting dirty and covered in puppy slobber would ruin the perfection his ex-partner tried to present to the world.

"I wouldn't move back. I'm more than happy just visiting." A thought struck him. "If you would consider it, you and Gypsy could fly out to Wyoming. We could have a few training sessions. Might be able to undo some of what Taylor did."

"Really?" Edward shot a shrewd glance over to where Randy now sat on the ground with the puppy in his lap and the little girl hanging over his shoulder. "Found something that makes you happy?"

"I found a lot of things that make me happy out there. Randy happens to be the most important." He stepped off the strides in between fences. "Are you going to count?"

Edward shook his head. "We won't make it out of the first round. Too many distractions and a damn open water jump." The rider flung his arm out to point at the offending jump. "Gypsy's scared of the water."

Les checked the water jump out—it was a huge ditch with a width of fourteen feet. It was the widest jump on the course and, if Gypsy spooked at water, there probably was no way Edward would be able to get him over it without unnerving the horse. He remembered the shows where he knew his horse didn't have what they needed to go clean. "Sorry, man."

"Were you serious about that offer for some training?" They went back towards the in-gate.

"Sure am. It'll be fun. I always enjoyed training."

Randy gave the little girl a hug and climbed to his feet as they approached.

"The earliest we'd be able to get out there would be December." Edward frowned. "Isn't it cold out there in December?"

"That's not a problem. We have a heated indoor arena. Randy, when are the finals this year?" Les ran his hand over his lover's shoulder as they followed Edward back to the stables.

"November thirtieth through to December ninth." Randy's eyes stayed on the horses as they passed them.

"Finals?" Edward grabbed a currycomb to start grooming Gypsy.

"Randy's a bareback bronc rider on the rodeo circuit out west. He's second in the standings and has a chance to win the championship at the national finals in Las Vegas." He chuckled at Randy's blush. "I wanted to make sure your coming out wouldn't mess with me going to watch him compete."

"Turning into quite the cowboy, I see." A cool voice came from behind them.

Stiffening, Les turned slowly to find Taylor standing in front of him. Les' tension relayed itself to Randy. His lover settled his hand on Les' lower back, giving him support while not intruding.

"Taylor," he said in a cold voice.

"Now, Leslie, is that the best you can do in greeting me?" Taylor moved in close and pressed a hard kiss to his mouth.

Les didn't back up or move in any way. He breathed in the expensive cologne Taylor used. There was a time when just the smell of that cologne would have made Les hard and horny, but now it left him empty. Randy's hand rubbed his back and he stepped into his lover.

Taylor smiled, but a puzzled look shone in his eyes. "I have to say Wyoming seems to agree with you, lover."

He didn't protest the endearment because he knew Taylor didn't mean it and never had. "Better than you ever did," he commented.

"Come now, Leslie. You know how terrible I am around sick people. I'm sensitive and all that pain just makes me weak." Taylor reached out to run a finger over his cheek. "Why don't we have dinner together after I win this class? Catch up on old times. Reconnect."

Resting against Randy, Les could feel the anger causing Randy's body to shake. He could tell his cowboy wanted to tell Taylor off, but was restraining himself for Les' sake.

"Sorry. I'm busy." Les started to turn back to Edward.

"I'm sure, now that you're back, you'd be interested in returning to Lourdin Stables. Maybe we can renew our partnership. We were good together." Taylor smiled at him, but his wink was for Randy.

"Why would you want a pathetic excuse for a man as your partner? I seem to remember you commenting on how, even if I recovered enough to eat and walk, I'd still be worthless. This dent in my head made me less of a man to you, not because you ever really loved me and just couldn't handle the thought of me being hurt. I was useless to you because I couldn't do all the work and train the horses you'd become famous for riding." Les poked Taylor in the chest.

Taylor's smile faltered, but he recovered to put a remorseful pout on his face. "Forgive me, lover. The trauma of watching that hack of a horse trample you caused my brain to short-circuit. I regretted my decision as soon as I stepped out of the room, but I didn't know how to get you to believe I'd changed my mind. So I thought I'd let you recover first and then we'd talk."

Edward snorted and Randy was barely holding in the laughter shaking his body. Les didn't take his eyes off his ex-lover.

"That's such a load of bullshit, Taylor. You waited six years to come find me and tell me you were sorry. What happened to the man you left me for? The whole man, who was perfect like I wasn't anymore." He felt his left arm start to tremble.

Randy moved up to stand beside him and Les slid his arm around Randy's lean waist. It was a way to ground him and to hide his weakness.

"He left Lourdin after two months, wasn't it?" Edward shot a questioning look at Taylor.

"Shut up, Monterrose," Taylor snarled.

"I remember it well. Very public break-up. McCarty stood in the middle of a crowded charity event and told everyone how self-centred and selfish Lourdin was. That Lourdin wouldn't know a good thing if it bit him on the ass. McCarty seemed fed up with doing everything and having Lourdin take all the credit. He also said Lourdin had a little prick." Edward seemed to be enjoying recounting the tale of Taylor's humiliation.

"Couldn't pull the wool over his eyes, huh? You didn't know how good you had it with me until you walked out. I mean, we were together for eight years and I never noticed just how egocentric you are, Taylor, and what an absolute asshole you can be when you don't get your way." Les studied the man who had been his first love.

There was a coldness to Taylor's golden good looks, as if he was staring at a statue. No wrinkles marred that perfect skin because Taylor never felt any sort of emotion—good or bad. His entire world centred on him and what he could get from others. Taylor didn't care if others loved him—he only wanted them to worship and adore him. He wanted them to hold him in awe. There wasn't any room for anyone else in Taylor's world.

"I must be the slowest person in the world. I never once saw that you were using me. When you left me, I was devastated. Even though everyone else saw you for what you really were, I loved you. I thought we were going to grow old together and raise horses." He laughed bitterly. "Luckily, I got hurt so you could leave me while I was still young, because you would have left me for someone younger when we got older."

Taylor started to say something, but Les stopped him with a shake of the head.

"No more bullshit, Taylor. I'm not coming back. I've got a ranch and a life in Wyoming. I'm living and I don't need you. From what I've heard, it sounds like you need me more."

Taylor sputtered. "The stables are doing fine. I don't know who's been telling you lies." A glare was shot towards Edward before Taylor focused back on Les. "He's just after you for your money. When he gets what he wants, he'll leave you too. No one wants to be seen with a deformed monster like you."

Les tightened his grip on Randy's waist as Randy lunged for Taylor. "He's not worth it, baby." He stared at Taylor. "Even if I believed Randy wanted me for my money, I'd still take that chance. You might have broken my heart, Taylor, but you didn't destroy it. You never had the power to do that."

"So what? You just came to show off your new boy toy then?" Taylor shrugged. "Whatever. I was the best you'll ever have and you'll never find anyone to replace me."

Les smiled and kissed Randy's cheek. "You were the best only because I didn't know any better. Now I know what the best is and, *lover*, you and your little prick don't measure up."

Edward burst out laughing, doubling over and holding his stomach. "Oh my God. Wait until I tell everyone McCarty was right. This will get me free drinks for a year."

Taylor snapped, "Well, this was the only time you'll hear me offer you a chance to come back. I don't know what I saw in you to begin with. You're *so* low class."

Taylor stalked off, his back ramrod straight. Edward supported his body against the stall door, still howling with laughter. The other riders stared at them as they walked their horses out of the stable area. Randy turned towards Les, staring deep into his eyes with a serious expression.

"I'm not after your money. Hell, Les, I don't even know how much money you have."

He cupped his smooth-shaved cheeks. "I know that, baby. Don't worry, we're okay." Turning back to Edward, he said, "You better let your groom finish saddling Gypsy for you. The class starts in a few minutes."

"Shit, watching your soap opera made me lose track of time." Edward reached into the windbreaker he had thrown over the wood wall. Pulling out two tickets, he handed them to Les. "You and Randy sit in these seats. They're right up front and you can watch Gypsy go. Maybe come up with some ideas I can try while we're doing the circuit. Also, it might be nice to know someone's rooting for me out there."

"Thanks."

* * * *

Halfway through the class, Randy leaned over and asked, "How much money do you have?"

Les had been waiting for that question. "You know all those rich people who were at the party on Thursday?"

"Not personally," Randy teased.

"I'm richer than two-thirds of them. My father founded a small investment firm that he'd developed into a multi-million dollar corporation by the time he died. I have very trustworthy and competent staff running it for me. I fly to New York once a month, on average, for the Board of Directors' meeting. If they need me before that, they know how to find me." He saw the shock glaze Randy's eyes.

"I guess that's why you can afford to take the rejects as payment for renting us the land." Randy frowned. "Are all the businesses you started out in Wyoming part of your father's company?"

"No. They're all mine. I don't plan on being majority owner of most of the new ones in a couple of years. They were something for me to do, since I couldn't show anymore. But, after talking to Edward, I think I've come up with a better idea."

"A better idea?" Randy's voice was low and Les knew he was still thinking about the money.

"Baby, does the money really matter?" He placed his hand on Randy's knee and squeezed.

"No, it doesn't. Just have to readjust my thinking, though. It would explain the private jet and buying a tailor-made tuxedo for your boyfriend." Randy moved closer to Les, letting Les rest on his body.

"Would you object to me opening up a training school at the ranch? Edward can pass the word. We'll have horses and riders coming in for sessions a week at a time. I'd make sure we were never jam-packed with people." He was a little worried about what Randy would say.

"First of all, it's your ranch. Do whatever you want to do. Second of all, if you feel up to it, do it. You were one of this sport's best riders, Les. Even if you can't compete anymore, you can still pass on what you learnt to make new riders better. Put you on a horse and you light up." Randy kissed his cheek. "I'll support you in anything you choose. Don't give up what you love."

"Thank you, love." Les kissed Randy's lips, putting all his love and happiness in the kiss.

Pulling apart, they settled back to watch the rest of the class. Les formed plans in the back of his mind while he explained the intricate rules of showjumping. There were no longer any thoughts of returning to Virginia. His ranch in Wyoming called to him, but the man sitting next to him spelt home.

Chapter Twenty-Six

Last night of the national finals rodeo

Les watched Randy pace their hotel room. He understood how nervous he had to be. Randy was in first place, but all it would take was him coming off his last horse to lose the championship. The odd thing was that, up until that night, the pressure hadn't seemed to affect Randy. He had laughed and joked with Tony and the other cowboys. He'd teased his sister about getting married in one of the drive-through wedding chapels littering the Vegas area. Tammy had teased him back, threatening to do just that. Jackson had paled, which had been an amazing feat in itself. Sister and brother had about busted a gut laughing at his foreman's reaction.

Randy walked past him. Reaching out, he snagged the man's belt loop and jerked him over to where he was sitting. Randy landed on his lap in a jumble of arms and legs. Wiggling and shifting, Les found he was on the bottom, lying on the couch with Randy pressed tight against him.

"You're tiring me out with all your pacing." Les cupped Randy's bubble ass, covered in sinfully tight jeans. Massaging those cheeks, he nibbled on Randy's bottom lip. "If you're nervous, I think I know of a way we can work off some energy."

"What does it involve?" Randy asked, his blue eyes shining.

"Us getting naked. Some sucking and, maybe, if you're good, some fucking."

He laughed at the speed with which Randy leapt to his feet. "Don't give yourself fabric burns getting those jeans off. We do have a little time before you need to be at the arena." Climbing to his feet, he started on his own clothes.

He finished unbuttoning his shirt, but he must not have been moving fast enough because a naked Randy knelt in front of him and started unfastening his pants. Shrugging off his shirt, he let the fabric fall off his shoulders. Not caring where it had landed, he ran his fingers through the dark curls on Randy's head. His pants were pushed down to his ankles and he stepped out of them.

"Ah," he groaned when he felt Randy's wet mouth settle around the flared head of his cock. "I see you're going to be a very good boy."

Randy's calloused hand fondled his balls while he sucked his cock down to the base. Les traced gentle lines over Randy's sunken cheeks as the man swallowed around him. He shivered when Randy's tongue licked a line up the throbbing vein along the underside of his shaft. Randy teased the sensitive spot just below the crown and tasted the pre-cum dripping from the slit in the head. He widened his stance to give Randy more access to his balls and his ass.

"Don't stop," he protested as Randy pulled off him.

"Where's the lube?"

Staring down at his lover, he couldn't think. All his mind could focus on was the glistening, swollen lips that had just surrounded him.

"Les, where's the lube?" Randy grinned up at him.

"Under the cushion in the couch." He gestured behind him.

"Of course, that's where we started and ended last night." Randy scrambled over there and dug under the cushion. "Ah-ha!" He held the tube up in triumph.

"Great. Now get back here and finish what you started." Les pouted.

Randy came back and placed a gentle kiss on Les' hip. "You know I won't leave you hanging."

Les' head dropped back as Randy deep-throated him again. The feeling of those muscles milking his cock drove him higher and higher. He barely noticed the pop of the top of the lube because he was focusing on not moving until Randy told him it was okay.

A cool, slick finger tapped against his hole causing him to thrust his cock farther into Randy's mouth. A happy hum vibrated around his shaft and he groaned. Randy's hand closed around his hip and tugged, letting him know that it was okay to move. He pulled back and Randy's finger slid into his opening.

"Shit," he mouthed as Randy twisted and caressed his gland.

Minutes later, he gave himself up to the intense feeling of being sucked and fucked at the same time. Randy's one finger became two and Les enjoyed the fullness, even though he knew there was more to come. His grunts and moans filled the air, along with the intoxicating scent of sex. A hot hand cupped his balls and played with them.

"Baby, gonna come soon," he warned.

Randy worked him harder, encouraging his climax. When he shot, stars exploded behind his eyelids and he could feel every particle of him empty into Randy's mouth. His lover drained the last drop of cum from him then licked him clean. Sinking to his knees, he kissed those swollen lips. He tasted the bitter saltiness of his own seed. His lover's cock bumped against his thigh and left a wet trail on his skin.

"Now for your reward. How do you want me?" Les knew it wouldn't take Randy long to come.

"Leaning over the couch." Randy helped him to his feet and took him around to the back of the couch.

Bracing his arms on the furniture, Les tilted his hips. He heard Randy's breath catch and Randy fondled Les' ass, working his thumb into Les' opening. He slid his other thumb in beside it, covered with more lube. Les rested his forehead on his arms and went with the sensations.

"Ready?" Randy brushed a kiss over the nape of his neck.

"Yes. Do me, baby."

The blunt head of Randy's cock rested at his opening for a moment, then he pushed in without stopping. They sighed when Randy's groin met Les' ass. He sent a prayer of thanks for them finally finding the time to go and get tested. Now there was nothing between them. Skin on skin and he could feel every inch of his lover.

He tightened his muscles and Randy's hands convulsed on his hips. His cowboy's control snapped and he found himself having to hold on to the back of the couch to keep from being slammed into it. Randy rode him hard and deep, but he didn't mind. He loved getting fucked like that.

"Oh shit," Randy cried out as his climax hit him.

Every muscle tightened and Les knew he'd have bruises on his hips from Randy's fingers. Wet heat filled him and he shivered.

A sweat-covered chest collapsed on his back. He could hear Randy breathing in his ear. Shifting his weight slightly, he eased the pressure on his left side but didn't move. He'd let Randy recover before he suggested they take a shower.

* * * *

Ten minutes later, Randy was whistling as he combed his hair. Les sat out on the couch, calling Tammy's room while he waited.

"Hello?" Jackson answered.

"Hey, we're heading down to the arena. Are you two going to show up a little later?" He glanced up to see Randy settle Les' cowboy hat on his head and wink at him.

"Yeah. We have some things to take care of before the round."

"No problem. You've got your tickets so we won't wait for you."

"See you there. Tell Hersch good luck." Jackson hung up.

"They're showing up a little later." He set the phone back in the cradle and tugged on the black hat brim. "That's my hat you're wearing."

"I know. Thought I'd wear it for good luck." Randy gave him a cheeky grin.

"I'll let you wear it this time, but you better not get it crushed." He pinched Randy's ass as the man walked out of the hotel room in front of him.

"Ouch." Randy shot a disgruntled look back at him.

"Hey, my idea worked, didn't it? You're not nervous anymore."

"You're right and I'm a lot more relaxed, which is good." Randy bumped shoulders with him as they waited for the elevator.

"Hersch. Hardin. You heading to the arena?" Tony joined them in the hallway.

"Yeah. You need a ride?" Randy smiled and tugged the brim at a lady stepping off the elevator.

"Yeah. Wanted to get over there a little early. Try to focus." Tony fidgeted with his belt buckle and his hat while they rode the elevator.

"Don't worry. You're firmly in first place. Even if you didn't cover your bull tonight, you'd still win," Randy reassured the bull rider.

"I know, but this is the biggest moment of my career so far. I'm thinking of just focusing on the PBR next year. That's where the real money is." Tony was talking about the Professional Bull Riders tour—all the top bull riders competed there for large purses, but they also got some of the rankest bulls.

"Let's make it through tonight and then you can decide." Les didn't want the man to be looking ahead when he still had to ride that night.

* * * *

Les stood up out of his seat. There weren't that many fans in the stands yet, but by the time the first event started, every seat in the arena would be filled. Rabid rodeo fans were dedicated and followed their cowboys all around the country to watch them ride. He'd dropped Randy and Tony off at the riders' entrance. His stomach was starting to turn somersaults. No matter how many big-time events he'd been at, he could never totally get rid of the nerves.

"Les Hardin?" a voice asked from behind him.

He turned and looked at the man standing a few feet from him. The brilliant blue eyes reminded him of someone—his mind was telling him he knew this guy.

"Yes."

A large hand was held out for him to shake. "My name's Rick Hersch. One of the riders pointed you out to me."

"No shit?" He shook Rick's hand.

"No shit, man. I was looking for Randy. They told me at the hotel he'd be here at the arena."

Les could see the resemblance between Randy and his older brother. Rick was a handsome man. *So that's what Randy will look like when he's older,* Les thought.

"He's getting ready to ride. He's competing in the bareback event." Les gestured to his seats. "Why don't we sit down and you can tell me what you're doing here?"

"I'd prefer to talk to Randy first. I know you're his lover, boyfriend or whatever. My old man made it quite clear about Randy's preferences. Still, this is family business. I'd like to talk to him and then he can decide what to tell you." Rick took a seat and rested his elbows on his knees.

"That's fine with me. How do you feel about Randy's relationship with me?" Les wondered if the oldest son shared the father's beliefs.

"Don't give a damn who he's fucking, to be honest with you. Just don't hurt him. Then we might have a problem." Rick gave him a direct look.

"Fair enough. Tammy will be here a little later."

Rick smiled. "It'll be old home week, I guess. I haven't seen them since they were little."

"Where did you go?" Les couldn't rein in his curiosity. "You don't have to tell me if you don't want to."

"It's okay. I actually went out to California. Our mother had some relatives out there Dad didn't like so it was the perfect place for me to stay. I hung out there until I graduated from high school. Then I joined the army. Been an army ranger for fourteen years. Plan to retire from the service." Randy's brother rubbed his hands together.

"You never tried to contact any of them?" Les didn't understand why he wouldn't try to get a hold of his family.

"Sure I did. I send a letter every three months, more if I know I'm being deployed."

"Randy didn't know." Les had a suspicious feeling he knew why.

"No one's answered them since Mom died, so I assume Dad's been throwing them away." Rick frowned.

Les looked up to see Tammy and Jackson coming down the stairs. "Brace yourself. Tammy's here."

Chapter Twenty-Seven

Randy eased down on the bronc. This was his chance to prove he was worthy of his father's respect. *Grow up,* he thought. Winning the championship wouldn't change his dad's opinion.

He took a deep breath and glanced up into the seats where Les had said he'd be sitting. He caught his lover's gaze and Les smiled at him. That smile, so full of love and pride, made it all worthwhile. Les winked at him and Randy knew everything would be okay. Les wouldn't leave him if he didn't win the buckle. Peace settled into his soul and he let the air out of his lungs. He wondered who the man sitting next to Les was.

He made sure his hat was pushed on tighter and nodded. The gate banged open. The bronc shot out and Randy marked him out perfectly. In one jump, he picked up the horse's rhythm and matched him buck for buck. The noise of the crowd, the smell of the dirt—everything faded away to the background. The only thing that existed for him was the horse. The stroke of the spurs from shoulder to withers. The creak of leather and the grunt of the bronc. Those were the only things he heard.

"Hersch," a voice broke through the zone he'd fallen into.

Lifting his head a little, he spotted the pick-up man riding next to him. The other rider was reaching out to unhook the flank strap. He got his hand free and bailed off the horse. He slid over the rump of the pick-up horse and landed on the arena floor. The roar of the crowd hit him like a wave of noise. He'd done it. There was no doubt in his mind. It had been the best ride he'd ever made.

Turning, he found Les in the stands. His lover was standing up, cheering and yelling. He waved to him and smiled. Randy couldn't wait to be alone with the man so he could taste that smile.

He made his way back to the chutes. As he was walking through one of the side gates, the announcer came over the loudspeaker.

"Eighty-eight point five, ladies and gentlemen. Randy Hersch has won the go-around and the world bareback bronc championship. Show him your appreciation."

Tony grabbed him around the waist, screaming and yelling. "You did it, man. That was the best ride I've ever seen you make."

"Thanks. I've got to find Les and Tammy." Randy hugged Tony hard. "Good luck on your ride. I know you'll win it."

"Thanks for reminding me. Say hi to Hardin. Hey, can I come and spend Christmas with you?"

Randy ran towards the riders' entrance, calling over his shoulder, "Sure. We'll see you whenever you show up."

He burst through the door and ran straight into the man he was looking for. Les' arms wrapped around his waist and crushed him to that muscular chest. He threw his arms around Les' neck, though he still remembered to hide the brush of his lips over Les' cheek.

"Oh, Randy, that was awesome." Tammy came squealing up to him and yanked him away from Les to give him her own bone-jarring hug.

"Good job, Hersch." Jackson slapped his back.

"Congratulations, Randy." A deep voice came from beyond the crowd of well-wishers.

He frowned. It sounded like his dad, but he knew his dad would never show up there. Les stepped out of the way and Randy felt his jaw drop.

"Rick?" he asked—the shock made him start.

"Yeah. You grew up, kid." His older brother smiled at him.

"Holy shit. What the hell are you doing here? Where the hell have you been?" Randy hugged his brother.

Rick looked over at Les. Randy shot Les a questioning glance.

"Let's go back to the hotel suite. You all can visit comfortably." Les touched the small of his back. "Do you need to stay?"

"Let me tell the officials I have to leave. I'll tell them it's a family emergency." He went to excuse himself from the ceremonies.

* * * *

Randy sat on the couch in his hotel suite, staring at his older brother. "So where have you been all these years?"

Les got up and gathered Jackson with a quick wave of his hand. "We'll leave to give you all some privacy."

"Fuck that. It's not like either of us is going to keep what's said here a secret from the people we love." Randy grabbed Les' hand and pulled him down to sit next to him. He challenged Rick to say anything.

"I wasn't sure how you felt about it, but it's fine with me if they stay." Rick rested his elbows on his knees and dangled his hands between his legs. "I went to California when I left the ranch. Since I joined the army, I've been everywhere."

"California. And you never once thought to let one of us know you were okay?" Randy felt the anger well within him.

Les squeezed his hand. "Give him a chance to talk, baby. I'm sure what he has to say will explain everything."

"Mom knew. She was the one who sent me to her relatives out there. I sent her letters every week."

"What was that? You couldn't even come back for her funeral?"

"I was in basic training and I didn't know about her death until a month afterwards. Dad didn't bother to inform any of Mom's relatives until months afterwards. It was too late. I've been back to visit her grave." Rick's eyes revealed the pain he still felt for missing his mother's funeral.

"But what about us, Rick?"

"There was nothing I could do. You were better off with Dad than you would have ever been with me. I moved from base to base, in country and out. I wrote every three months, but I never got a response." His brother rubbed his face.

"I think your father was probably throwing the letters out," Les interjected.

Randy thought about it for a moment. Les was more than likely right. It was something his dad would do. "So why look us up now? And why come to Las Vegas instead of the ranch?"

"I got a strange rambling letter from Dad the other day, along with some papers from his lawyer. It seems since you're a queer and Tammy is fornicating with a black man—his words, not mine," Rick said when Jackson growled, "he's disinherited both of you and left everything to me. I guess just running away from home puts me a little above y'all."

"After everything I've done for the bastard, he stabs me in the back." Tammy jumped to her feet and paced.

"I'm not surprised he threw me out of the will. Why do you suppose he hates us so much? Are we not his real children?"

Les encircled his shoulders and Randy rested his head on his lover's chest.

Rick chuckled. "No, we're his all right. Every one of us has his eyes. Dad is just one of those people who hate. They're so filled with rage at their lives and the world that it boils over in anger and hatred. None of us did anything more to him than draw breath." Rick sat up straight and looked them all in the eye. "I want to tell you what I plan on doing."

Randy found he didn't care what Rick planned on doing with the ranch. It wasn't home for him—it hadn't been home for a very long time, no matter how much he'd dreamt of returning there in triumph. He snuggled closer to Les and closed his eyes.

"I have no interest in running the ranch. Part of the problem Dad had with me was the fact that I didn't love the ranch like he did. I'm offering to let you both buy in as partners after Dad dies."

"He'll live forever just to spite us," Tammy mumbled.

They laughed but Randy had the tired feeling she just might be right.

"You and Tammy can run the ranch, Randy. I only need to know I have a place to come back to when I retire from the army in a couple years."

Tammy didn't hesitate. "I'll take you up on that offer. I've been running the ranch pretty much on my own for a while now." She turned to Jackson. "Will you still love me when I'm a prosperous ranch owner?"

Jackson kissed her deeply and for a very long time.

"I think that's a yes," Rick teased. He turned his gaze to Randy. "Well, brother, you always loved that ranch more than I ever did."

Randy glanced up to find Les staring down at him.

"Whatever you decide, baby. I'll back you," Les whispered.

"You know that old adage, 'Home is where the heart is'?"

Les nodded.

"I believe it's true." He faced his brother and said, "I appreciate the offer, but I'm going to turn it down."

"What?" Tammy whirled on him. "How can you say no? You've always wanted to run the ranch."

"I did, but then I met someone who taught me dreams can change. When they change, you don't lose them, the dreams just get bigger and better. I'll be training horses, just a mile or two down the road. If you'll have me?" He moved back a few inches to be able to see Les' face clearly.

"My home is yours, for as long as you want to live there." Les cupped his face. "I love you, Randy."

Tears welled in his eyes. "I love you, too," he managed to get out around the lump in his throat.

Standing up, Rick ushered Tammy and Jackson out of the suite. "We'll catch up with you tomorrow."

Randy didn't even register the door shutting. He was swimming in the love he saw in Les' eyes. They climbed to their feet and went into the bedroom. In silence, they undressed each other. They held hands while they lay side by side on the bed.

The kisses were gentle and the loving was slow. He was on his back when Les filled him. Passion built with each thrust of Les' hips and pump of his hand. His climax caught him by surprise. He closed his eyes and moaned as he came hard. Les climaxed seconds after he did.

After catching his breath, he rolled so they were lying on their sides, facing each other. He touched the scar and the dent with soft fingers.

"I'm quitting the rodeo. Tonight was my last ride," he confessed.

"Are you sure?"

He knew Les didn't doubt him. His lover wanted to make sure he was positive about his decision.

"Yeah. I decided right before the finals, win or lose, this was going to be my last rodeo. I never loved it. Not like Tony does. I love you and I don't like being away from you. So I'll be staying at the ranch. Do you think you can stand being with me all the time?"

"I think I can find some things to keep you busy," Les flirted.

"Good. It's time for me to go home, love, and I want my home to be with you."

"Always and forever, baby."

Randy tugged the covers over them and cuddled close to his partner. Les was the man he was determined to love for the rest of his life. He listened to Les' slow breathing and he smiled. He was on top of the rodeo world, but, more than that, he was finally going home.

About the Author

There is beauty in every kind of love, so why not live a life without boundaries? Experiencing everything the world offers fascinates TA and writing about the things that make each of us unique is how she shares those insights. When not writing, TA's watching movies, reading and living life to the fullest.

T.A. Chase loves to hear from readers. You can find her contact information, website details and author profile page at http://www.total-e-bound.com.